WYD
WISH
YOU
DEAD

THE FIRST IN THE LEGACY SERIES

DAN ANDERSEN

WYD Wish You Dead
Copyright © 2021 by Dan Andersen

Tellwell Talent
www.tellwell.ca

ISBN
978-0-2288-4769-4 (Hardcover)
978-0-2288-4768-7 (Paperback)
978-0-2288-4770-0 (eBook)

Table of Contents

Chapter 1. The Journey Home 1

Chapter 2. Paper and Mag 9

Chapter 3. Brother Time...20

Chapter 4. Intel Swell 30

Chapter 5. The Big Meet..59

Chapter 6. The Guard Comes Down 118

Chapter 7. The Break-In..127

Chapter 8. Miss Guided 135

Chapter 9. Bad Things...145

Chapter 10. Chase 175

Chapter 11. Talisman 213

Chapter 12. The Answer...231

1

The Journey Home

In the middle of night, in the pouring, sticky Pensacola rain, a black-and-silver twin-engine Cessna 441 sits on the tarmac with its engines running. There are only four passengers aboard the poorly lit cabin. Halfway back by a window seat, a man in his late sixties sits. He wears a dark sports jacket and a black Mandarin-collared shirt buttoned to the top. His cell phone goes off in the pocket of his jacket. He pulls it out with his right hand, revealing a rune stone thumb ring.

His cell illuminates his well-groomed short facial hair. His eyes are locked on the incoming text message from a contact with the initials "NB":

REJSEGUIDE GONE! Coutts and Sherwood are dead.
SHE TOOK THEIR HANDS!

The man presses Copy on the message and pastes it onto a message to "WA." He turns his phone off and slowly looks out the window at the rain as the plane starts to move. The man notices a piece of paper sticking out of the map pocket in the seat in front of him. He reaches over slowly and pulls it out. It's folded three times from top to bottom, beside a yellow pencil. He opens it and reads it by the light coming through the window. It says: "Nine-Day Travel Guide."

An hour later in a small warm hotel room in Reno, Nevada, Trace Scott sits on the side of the bed and makes a call from her cell phone. She gently smiles and says in a smooth voice, "I'll be home tomorrow," to which the older woman on the other end of the phone replies, "I can hardly wait!" She ends the conversation with a sigh and a simple "'Night."

"Goodnight, Mom," Trace responds, pausing for a moment. She then slowly walks into the washroom wearing a grey T-shirt and underwear. The place is dimly lit. Her walk and silhouette are smooth. She has a scar on her right wrist from a raccoon bite when she was a kid. Her long dark hair falls between her shoulder blades. She returns from the washroom and turns off the lights then crawls under the covers. She pulls them up just under the curve of her arm. There is a pitter-patter against the windowpane as an evening rain begins, and the echo of a V8 car as it leaves the parking lot.

She gets out of bed and walks slowly to her motel room door, which has come ajar. The deliberate *click* is felt in her hand as the door closes. She turns her head to the side and looks out the corner of the window as the thoughts in her mind go down with the glow of the moon, then she idly returns, lost in thought, to the side of the bed. A gentle breeze rises from the low-humming air-conditioning unit, moving the dove-grey curtains.

An unfamiliar feeling comes over her as she crawls into bed; the idea of sleeping alone, strange. She tosses back and forth, and arranges the pillows in the shape of a crescent moon. Curling up slowly, she comes to rest on her right side and closes her eyes.

The moon and the sun pass each other like strangers on the highway, and suddenly it's a crisp and humid morning. The asphalt is shining after the rain. It's a warm, sunny June day, with the temperature approaching 75°F. A silver Mercedes 6.3 convertible with a red interior and ragtop growls as it crests the windy, twisty mountain horizon with the top down. The sun is high, casting shadows on the right side of Trace's neck. She's wearing a teal-coloured T-shirt with "Olds Grizzlys" written across the chest. The ends of her hair are blowing around her face, touching her lips, brushing the corners of her mouth, flipping around the rims of her sunglasses. One Republic is playing loud on the radio.

Trace Scott is thirty-seven, born on St. Patrick's Day. She is a striking five foot six with warm green eyes and long brown hair. She has a nose piercing on her left side. She's always listening to music: it's her drug. Presently, she's heading to her childhood home in the small town of Coldstream, Washington. She left New York, where she was an investigative journalist at the *Pillar and Post*. Her knack was profiling all her subjects in detail before writing articles. She honed her skill for getting people to talk by staying on the right side of being intrusive.

Trace is divorced from Jerome Mercer, an owner of a successful trucking company, a workaholic driven by his own goals: a good man, but married to his businesses. Their business and careers drove them apart. She's frugal to a fault and received a fair, comfortable settlement from her ex.

As Trace drives through the mountains, her thoughts turn back to her youth and she starts daydreaming of the time she spent fishing with her father and grandfather and baking bread with her mother in the kitchen. Things were pure and simple then. She would sometimes throw a ball with her brother, Brian, in the backyard between the hammock and the veranda. Her golden retriever, Pax, would run around the yard chasing missed balls and soap bubbles. Brian is thirteen years her senior.

Trace now descends into the valley leading to Coldstream. The smells and the visuals of the beautiful valley and lake are in front of her. This arid valley is full of orchards and small wineries. Twenty-five miles away is the city of Mason, which is primarily a retirement community and the second home for oil and gas executives who have built large homes in the city along the one-hundred-mile stretch out at Nichol Lake. Over a bridge and around two corners, Trace comes to the town's first set of lights. As she stops, she glances both ways at the construction and development that was not there when she left. It's been five years. As she sits at the light and waits for it to turn green, a copper Audi R8 Spyder turns into her lane, just before it changes. She follows it down the hill through three more sets of lights, then watches as it turns left at the bottom of the hill in front of her. Three more sets of lights past the hospital, over the hill and she turns off. Less than two miles down and one block off the lake stands the white stone two-story house where she was raised: it sits back from the road on a large ten-acre lot. Only two posts remain where the gate and fence used to be. She drives slowly into the driveway. It is as if time is standing still.

The power top on her car comes up and she turns the car off. From the south side of the house comes a beautiful green-eyed older woman. Helen Scott, five foot six and one hundred and forty pounds, is wearing a translucent white sundress with green spaghetti straps that shows the outline of her breasts and nipples. Her long brunette hair is in a ponytail. The left side has come undone with slight traces of grey appointed throughout. They walk toward each other, smiles growing. The warm breeze blows off the lake from the south, sideways, whipping their hair and kissing their noses. There are simultaneous sighs.

"Oh . . . look at you!" Helen says.

With a smirk and a chuckle Trace says, "Mom, the girls are out!" as she glances down at her mother's unsecured top.

"Give me a hug." Helen initiates a maternal embrace. "You're beautiful!"

"I missed you, Mom," Trace murmurs.

"Let's go in," Helen says and Trace gently nods. From inside the house comes the sound of an excited large dog. As they stroll toward the porch, Helen grabs her sundress with her right hand. Just then, the solid black German shepherd comes bounding out the open door toward them, his tail wagging. He sits upright barely three feet in front of them. "I call him Benjamin," Helen states. "He's only seven months old."

Trace goes down on one knee. She grabs Benjamin's ears with both hands. "You're beautiful!" she says. She glances up and notices, on the veranda, the back of a man's grey-haired head facing the other way, where he sits in a partially refinished grey-and-brown oak kitchen chair. She stands up after petting Benjamin and the dog releases in the other direction.

Both women continue toward the house, talking in a soft girlfriend tone about the garden off to the left. As Helen points, Benjamin prances across the grass, grabs a stick and runs on to the veranda. Helen slows her gait. Trace puts her left foot on the first tread of the steps, and says a drawn-out "Da-a-a-d." Her instinctive training and intuitive investigative nature notices everything in a glance. Her pride in her father's craftsmanship warms her and she's keen on his accomplishments.

"Hey," the man replies as he rises from the chair with a big smile. Arthur Scott is fit, six foot one, two hundred and twenty pounds, a ruggedly handsome sixty-five-year-old man with grey hair and green eyes. He's wearing a grey Beatles T-shirt and white knee-length cargo shorts. He raises his arms. They embrace. As he gently grabs her by both shoulders with his hands, he looks at her and says, "Who are you, and where is my little girl?"

"It's been a while, hasn't it, Dad," she says as he stares directly into his eyes. He opens the door and Trace and Helen file in, with Arthur following behind them and closing the door.

Across the open-concept room at the other end of the house is the kitchen, copper pots and pans hanging above the island. The interior has white-trimmed baseboards, crown molding and banisters, with a grey tile floor in the entryway that leads past the living room area into the dining room area where the hardwood begins. A dark brown leather sofa and matching chairs separate the dining room from the living room. Behind that, on the right, is a white encased fireplace with a sixty-inch television mounted above it. The office directly under the stairs is painted medieval bronze with a four-foot-square chalkboard that states "Believe in Tomorrow." Off to the left, just before the dining room, is the staircase leading upstairs. The wall behind the staircase has been painted terracotta, matching the oven hood in the kitchen. State-of-the-art stainless steel appliances with bright red knobs adorn the kitchen.

Trace takes five steps in, while her parents remain stationary, their hands at their sides. She slowly turns three hundred and sixty degrees and says, "Whose house is this? Wow!"

Arthur shuffles his feet and with his hands still at his sides, he looks up at Trace and says, "I've had quite a bit of time on my hands these days since retirement."

Helen, a country girl, strides into the kitchen and as she does, she picks up a tennis ball with her right hand that was on the floor at the landing of the stairs. She approaches the island and says with a rasp in her voice, "You have a choice between chicken and chicken."

"As long as I get potatoes I'm good to go," Arthur says. He turns to walk out the door and adds, "Here's where you girls bond for a bit. Need me to get your things from your car?"

"It's okay," Trace tells him. "I'll grab them after supper." He quickly nods his head, gently smiles and walks out the door.

Later that evening, Trace and Helen sit at the island with a glass of wine. Remnants of supper sit on the table. Arthur lounges in the adjoining living room with a bottle of Tuborg beer. "Has Brian found that magical woman yet?" asks Trace, not sounding coy.

"Same old Brian," replies her mom. "You look tired. You should go grab some sleep," she adds.

"I have to go clean up," says Trace.

"If you mean dishes, forget about it," Dad says as he strides over, grabs a couple of plates and heads to the kitchen. "Your bags are in your old room. I painted it and it has a brand-new queen-size bed," he says.

Trace and Helen stand up and hug each other warmly. With a sigh, Trace turns and gives a gentle stretch. "A bath sounds good," she says. The openness of the house echoes as they all say goodnight and Trace climbs the stairs. She listens to the sound of her mom and dad doing the dishes in the background while she undresses. As far back as she can remember Trace has always taken off her left sock first. Her pants lie folded on the chair beside the bed now, as she walks into the bathroom removing her shirt. There's a squeak of the hot water tap followed by the sound of running water. Steam escapes from the crack under the door. She lights some candles, turns off the lights and sinks into the hot bath, giving herself over to the soothing water.

2

Paper and Mag

It's nine o'clock in the morning in downtown Detroit. On the sixteenth floor in an old concrete office building, two women sit facing each other across from a modern cherry-wood-and-ivory desk. One of them is a lawyer with medium-length black hair, high cheekbones and hazel eyes: Janice Breaker. The other woman is wearing casual grey slacks and a black windbreaker with a fitted white T-shirt underneath. Her long blond hair is pulled back through a black Detroit Tigers ball cap. The office is tastefully adorned with artwork from Asia. The sunlight shines on the wall behind the lawyer, just over her shoulders.

"You need to find a way out of this before we all go down," says Janice.

"Screw that noise. I'm not gonna take you down. Piss me off, and I'll make you disappear," replies the woman, whose name is Elon.

"We're done here! I'm not going down with you and I'm not going anywhere. Don't write me. Don't phone me. I don't know you," says Janice.

Elon replies as she stands up, "One dead bitch asset attorney—you think anybody's gonna care?"

She briskly leaves the office through the teak-trimmed glass door. Janice stares across the room and notices something on the chair next to where the woman sat. A few minutes pass by as she watches the door slowly close. She gets up from her chair and walks around her desk and looks down. A ripped crossword puzzle sits unfinished on top of a deep-blue shoebox. She places the crossword puzzle on her desk and opens the shoebox slowly. It reveals a black bra and a man's bloody left hand with a wedding band on it. Just then the phone rings. She stares out the window as she answers the phone.

"Have I got your attention?" Elon says.

At seven-thirty a.m., eighteen hundred miles west, just outside the city of Mason, two men, Book, an elderly man with a full head of grey hair, and Eddie, a large man in his forties with lobster-like hands, are standing at the rear of their similar white Ford trucks. Book stands staring and assessing the damage after he backed into Eddie's truck. Both of the trucks suffer damage. The left side of each bumper is lifted up as if it were waving at low-flying aircraft. The men are friends. They purchased their trucks together.

Ed Henry is on his cell phone. "Odan, you're not going to believe this. Book just backed into my truck. Now we're going to have to call Gary. Can you believe that shit?" Almost shouting, Odan replies, "He has a back-up camera. How in the hell did that happen?"

Ed comes back with, "He was on the phone with Ruby and you know how flustered he gets when he's trying to talk on the phone and drive. I was distracted by a call from Deb. She was babbling about those new books you're writing, something about *Playing with a Broken Moon* and *The Taste* . . . anyways . . . I wasn't paying a lot of attention. Book and I were just going to swap some cherries that I brought back from the farm."

Odan replies calmly, "You know, of course, that Gary's going to piss himself. Imagine how funny that's going to look—two almost identical trucks, including the kiss-my-ass marks on the bumpers, driving back into town."

"I'm calming down now . . . do you have time for a coffee or a beer later in the day?" asks Ed.

Odan replies with a sigh. "Four o'clock works for me, where we met last."

"You're on. I'll see you there," says Ed.

Ed waves to Book who is already in his truck as both men start their vehicles and drive away. Another twenty-five miles away, the sound of race cars' exhaust is bouncing off the concrete retaining wall in front of the grandstand. Six cars are practicing doing hot laps. Odan, a tall, handsome, blond forty-something, wearing wraparound sunglasses, tight-fitting jeans, expensive shoes and an untucked, tight-in-the-chest shirt, stands in the skybox on his cell phone. Years of dedication to fitness and the love of the outdoors have chiselled him. His strong jawline, inviting warm blue eyes and colourful personality have made him popular with the ladies. The male voice on the other end of the line says, "Two-sixty-two is on its way . . . over you, and landing in ten."

Odan replies back in a stern voice, "I've got a four o'clock back in Mason." He puts his cell phone back on the clip on his right hip. It rings again seconds later. He notices the call comes from a blocked number. He pushes Accept and brings the phone to his left ear.

"Bad things are coming. Bad things are coming. I wish I was there," the male voice on the other end says.

"Who is this? What do you want and where are you calling from?" Odan clearly states as he removes his sunglasses and turns his body slowly counterclockwise. He says it again. "Who is this?"

The voice on the other end says, "Soon."

They both hang up. Odan walks down to his black Ford truck parked behind the grandstand. He fires it up and the V8 Coyote engine growls. He sits waiting. Flying over the truck and about to land is the world's largest helicopter, an Mi-26. It lands in the racetrack's parking lot in front of him. Odan gets out, but leaves the engine running as he approaches the landed helicopter. Three men get out, now only ten feet away. As the rotors of the helicopter are spinning about, the man on the far right says, "Seems to work just fine. We're having some issues with the pickup, though. The pump has cavitation problems."

Odan replies with a smile, "Do you know what I'm going to say next?"

"Yeah . . . hahaha. If you go up in the air, I know you're going to fix it, and we're all going to have to eat crow at the end of the day," says the tall thin man in the middle. "I've got so much stuff to do. I can't believe you guys are here just to get a little insight on how to fix this," says Odan.

After a short discussion, the crew turn around and walk back toward the helicopter. The helicopter gently rises straight upward and tilts forward then flies away. On his way back to his truck, Odan receives another call.

"You're not going to be late for our four o'clock, are you?" the voice on the other end asks.

"Not a hope in hell," Odan retorts.

"Is Ranger going to be there?" the other asks.

"Oh yes, he will be. He's not going to miss this opportunity," says Odan.

Meanwhile, miles away, Trace is driving west from Coldstream on her way to Mason. Her top is down on her car. Her makeup is done and her hair is in a ponytail. She's wearing a royal blue blazer with her dad's black Beatles T-shirt underneath and tight-fitting jeans. Trace pulls into Mason. She drives along a twisted boulevard and passes through a series of traffic lights. She stops at the red light. She's two cars back behind a black-and-silver Bentley convertible with a cream top. She creeps up on the Bentley's rear bumper before the light turns green. The light changes and the Bentley speeds away.

After two blocks, it turns into a parkade on the left. She drives ahead, looking left and right for a place to park in front of a two-story commercial glass building on the edge of the lake. She pulls a U-turn and pulls into a spot close to the glass building's front doors. She checks her mirrors before opening her door and climbs out slowly. She glances up at the marble sign above the glass doors stating, "Naramata." She walks across the two-tone grey opaque marble-tile floor to where a tall bleach-blond woman stands smugly behind a reception counter; she is possibly in her early forties, wearing a tight-fitting red sundress with black spaghetti straps, and stilettos. Trace quickly glances at her sleek physique before they speak. The woman has surgically enhanced lips and breasts. Their eyes connect. Trace is caught glancing, yet keeps her smirk held within. The woman asks, "Can I help you?" with a straightforward demeanour.

"I have an appointment to see Mr. Adelle," says Trace in a clear, confident tone, wrinkling her nose and dragging her right index finger slowly in front of her on the reception desk.

Just then, the oak doors in front of her open and a tall, bald, older man with glasses walks out. "You must be Trace Scott," the man states coarsely, in his French accent. He extends his hand and shakes hers firmly. "I've heard so much about you," he continues, smiling.

"Likewise, I've heard so much about you, Mr. Adelle," she says as they begin walking toward a steel staircase.

"Call me Gary," he states in a friendly tone. "I knew it was you," he says. There's a delay as she thinks and stares. "You were driving the Mercedes that was crawling up my ass at the red light."

"You were the one in the Bentley dragging your ass?" she asks. He turns and smiles, showing his bright white teeth with a silver cap as they climb the final step and turn right into his office. There are floor-to-ceiling windows on the west side of his office overlooking the lake. He walks around a white modern contemporary desk with a tasteful chrome model aircraft on it. There are two black computer monitors on the desk butted up together. The keypads are

WYD WISH YOU DEAD

underslung at the centre of the desk. The walls are done in light-red earth tone. An archery bow is leaning against a corner chair. Two pictures of raging fires decorate the right-hand wall. The teak shelving units reveal pictures of one boy and one girl, both teenagers.

He walks around his desk and as he sits, he asks, "What brings you to Mason?"

"A career change and . . . of course, I got divorced and my family lives here, but you know all that." Their eyes lock and she stares at him for a brief moment. The mood becomes very soft. There are minutes of silence; she looks down on his desk and sees four books overlapping each other by the bottom corners, displayed like a fan. The bottom three books are about Porsche cars; the top one is titled *Biltong* by J. Rundle. Casually, she grips her right hand under the front of his desk and slowly points to the novel. She asks with a coyote smile, "What is that about?"

Another delay as they both look at each other and out the window.

"It's about a murder . . . actually, a serial killer," he states and continues. "There is a story that I would like to get, but I haven't been able to get close to the guy for the better part of . . . many years. The story is about an inventor, author and dreamer. He has written fiction books. He's written some pretty good romance and children's novels, too. Have you heard of *Playing with a Broken Moon*, *The Taste* or *Penguin Loves Bear*? Those are some of his. My wife loves his shit. He's had some tough times and he's been local for the better part of six or seven years. The whole story reeks of the unknown. You get the story and you got the job. There is a long list of people that quote, unquote 'fucked him over,' including the courts. He was involved in a month-long trial. It's as simple as that," Gary states, trying to keep calm and playful while watching her every move.

Trace asks in a polite, straightforward tone, "Sorry, I've never heard of him. Who is the subject . . . and when do I start?"

"His name is Odan, and, by the way, some say I threw him under the bus years ago. You get the story and I'll put you under contract to do a half a dozen stories over the next two years." He slides her an envelope on the table that has cash in it and says, "Two weeks, three weeks tops . . . every opportunity has a shelf life, Ms Scott."

The room is quiet as she walks back and forth in front of the window looking at the sailboats crossing the bay. "I'll get it, but only if I get to know what you did to him." She pauses before she continues. With a half-condescending glare she looks at the envelope on the table and says sharply and politely, "No, on the other hand, I don't want your opinion. I'll find out for myself. And why . . . you—you of all people—why you would pay me cash." She leaves the envelope on the table. She walks to the door and opens it very quietly, but closes it hard behind herself.

Vancouver, Canada. A man sits at a parkade booth. A woman drives up in a tan Chevy Malibu rental car. She rolls down her window, with the car still moving. Just as the man begins to greet the woman, she pulls out a Glock 34 handgun with a suppressor and shoots him through the glass of the booth. The bullet pierces through the man's right eye. Blood splatters upward across the glass as he collapses like an accordion to the ground. She drives through the barricade arm, shattering it into hundreds of pieces, and a severed piece scratches against the driver's door, peeling paint all the way to the rear fender. The squelch of the car's fan belt and squeal of the tires echo through the parkade. She pulls her car up into the second level. She looks over at four open files on the seat beside her. The files are marked *"Asset Pedofie"* in German handwriting and a picture matching the lot attendant on top. She gets out of the car, throws a lit match on the files and locks the car. The car smokes, smoulders and blows up. She doesn't flinch or change her gait as she walks down the ramp dressed in a black windbreaker and grey Stepchild turtleneck, Detroit Tigers ball cap, gloves, sunglasses and military-style grey slacks. A man in his forties dressed in a black suit and grey T-shirt approaches her from her left, halfway down the ramp.

"Ma'am, there seems to be a fire up there," he states in an orderly German voice. "That's okay, I'm leaving and you're not," she says as she turns and faces him less than four feet away.

"Pardon me?" he asks, tilting his head backward as he approaches even closer. She tosses the car keys in the garbage, and with her right hand, she reaches in her pocket and pulls out a cell phone. She pushes a button on the cell phone and "Anant" is displayed. It rings and connects.

"Where is he?" she asks. She says it three more times before the female voice on the other end replies, "I'll get back to you."

"No, you won't. You have eighteen hours and I'll call you," she says and hangs up. She pulls the SIM card out of the cell, breaks in half between her two fingers and tosses them both in the garbage can. She turns to greet the man when he sticks out his right hand, then she quickly grabs and twists the man's wrist with her left hand. He falls to the concrete; the right side of the man's head bounces off the bumper of a red parked truck. The man grabs his head as blood drips to the concrete and starts to pool. She bends over slowly, making a wedge fist with her right hand, not losing eye contact with the man. Her face gets within a foot of his face. It tightens and tenses as she throws a quick decisive blow to his throat.

The man gasps for air, grabbing his throat, and asks, "Who are you?"

"It doesn't matter who I am. All you need to know is I'm sending a message and ridding the world of a disease-infected *arschficker*." She grabs a long knife out of the sheath on her right hip. She slowly drags the metal across the concrete floor in front of him. The blood starts to gather at the sleeve of his dress jacket. She places her left glove over his mouth firmly and runs the knife from his groin up to his chest. Blood escapes the man's body, squirting upward three inches in two places just below his ribcage. He rolls over onto his left side, shaking. She slowly stands up and stands over the body until it stops quivering. Bending over, she cleans her knife off, pressing firmly down on the man's blazer. She reaches inside his blazer and grabs a key attached to a small lanyard with the number four on it. Then she turns and strides down the exit ramp, putting her knife away and removing her gloves. She slowly opens the door to the ticket booth, revealing the man collapsed inside like an octopus out of water. She notices a lanyard on the very bottom shelf tucked away in a ball and grabs it. She shuffles her clothing to completely conceal the Glock in the small of her back, then crosses the road with no traffic in sight. She walks into the sun on the side of the street. She pauses to feel its warmth and drifts away into a past time.

3

Brother Time

Trace pulls up to a little coffee shop called The Grind in Mason. She throws her blazer onto the passenger seat. Just before she grabs the handle on the door, she notices what looks to be three white company trucks parked to her left beside each other. Two of the trucks have damaged rear bumpers. As she enters and turns to the right, she gazes around the well-lit room that is scattered with earth-tone pictures and artifacts of the '60s and '70s. She walks up to the coffee bar and stares at the menu board for a moment before an attractive blond-haired girl in her twenties asks, "What can I get you?"

"I'll have the turkey club croissant, oh . . . can you make it a combo, please, with a coffee?"

"Sure," the girl replies. "That will be six-thirty, please." Trace inserts her bank card in the machine and punches in a series of numbers. "Your coffee will be on the end of the counter and I'll bring your food out to you when it's up," the girl says with a smile, pointing to her right.

As she picks up her coffee and approaches the condiment table, Trace notices over her shoulder, through the window, a dark-grey Chevy SUV pull into the parking lot. She finishes adding cream to her coffee and sees a middle-aged blond man step out of the SUV. As he's walking up to the coffee shop door, she seats herself by the window. He's wearing a blazer and khaki pants. The bulge on his right hip exposes a gun holster. He says to the girl behind the till, "I'll have a tall coffee, please and thank you." The girl behind the till says nothing. He places some change on the counter and he walks to the end of the service bar. As he grabs his coffee, he glances to the other end of the restaurant. He walks briskly over to the condiment island. As he adds cream and a package of sweetener to his coffee, he slowly looks up and then back down again. Clearly having something on his mind, he walks over to where Trace is sitting.

"Is this seat taken?" he says in a stern voice, looking her directly in the eyes.

"I guess it is now," Trace replies. He sits and places his coffee cup right in front of him and then slowly moves it to the right, out of his way. He leans forward and puts his forearms on the table. Just then, the blonde from behind the counter brings out Trace's food. As she places the food on the table, the man looks out the window avoiding eye contact with the staff member.

After she leaves, he resumes his position with his forearms on the table. With a straight face he asks, "What brings you to this town? I mean, what the hell are you doing here?"

Trace replies, "Not till you tell me what's going on with you and that server."

"We used to see each other. She lost a child that she claimed was mine," he says quickly, but in a regretful tone. They both now smile. Trace puts down her sandwich, they stand up and he surrenders a big aggressive hug. He grabs her head with both of his hands and kisses her forehead. When they take their seats again, a warm feeling comes over Trace. "I missed you, sis," Brian says.

"I miss everything about you except for that damn gun," she replies.

"I heard you were home. I got a call yesterday from Mom."

"Mom's got a big mouth," Trace says. "I wanted to surprise you."

"So, tell me about your new job, and that's just because I don't want to pry into what went wrong in New York . . . or do I?" he asks casually.

She looks outside and watches a couple more white pickup trucks pull into the parking lot and she says, glancing back at him, "We grew into friends and before you know it, we were closer to our work than we were to each other. We talked for years and years about having kids and that white picket fence . . . and the closer we got to having that, it seemed we forgot all about it. We grew apart from each other. Shit, I don't even know him anymore."

Staring at her while she bites into her croissant, Brian says, "That doesn't tell me anything about your new job and why you're here. All we get is phone calls on special occasions, so please tell me if I've done something wrong . . . or maybe it's you that's done something wrong. Three years is a long time."

Trace begins to ramble, "It's nothing like that and yet everything like that . . . it was all about work." She pauses. "My life just became all about deadlines and who was doing who. I got so wrapped up that I couldn't remember who I was. Coming home was . . . odd, but it felt warm. It seemed like I lived in a place full of sparks . . . and yet there were none in my life. Forget three years. It seems like I've lost a decade."

"You left like a little kitten and you came back like a tiger," Brian says.

With a quaint smile she replies, "Fuck you, Brian. I went to private school and college." They continue to talk. "So, I got a job, at least . . . I think I got a job," she says. "What?" he says.

"I'm supposed to get a story on a guy named Odan for *Naramata*," she tells him as she turns her head.

"That's really funny." He lowers his voice. "Whatever you do . . . don't look over your shoulder," Brian says, "because he's behind you at the corner table."

She slowly turns her head and views a group of people sitting in the corner. She turns to her brother, leans across the table and asks in a quiet tone, "Which one is he?" "He's the blond one in the blue shirt," he replies.

"Do you know the other people at the table?" she asks.

"The guy on the far left, with the glasses . . . I think his name is Robert Barnes. The guy next to him, hmm, green shirt . . . is Gary Wallace. He owns a body shop in Coldstream. The guy in the plaid shirt, with the John Deere ball cap . . . I'm not sure what he does, but I think his name is Alan. The Black gentleman, his name is Ryan. He's an ex-professional football player of some sort. I think he works for Odan. The guy with the moustache in the white golf shirt is a banker, I think. I don't know his name, could be Walter. The guy with the glasses and the grey hair . . . his name is Raymond. He's a shrewd businessman here. Odan calls him 'RO.'"

Brian takes a second to sit back and she sighs. She looks at a man outside giving his dog some water at the back of his pickup truck. She then glances across the road to see a family loading fruit into their minivan from a fruit stand. Slowly, with purpose, she stares back at her brother and asks in a sharp tone, "Is there a story here or is it just a bunch of hillbillies hanging out?"

He takes a little time as he plays with the tines of his fork. "They're just some ordinary people going about their daily business, trying to forget things that have gone wrong . . . especially the one you're trying to get a story about," he says. Trace notices from a reflection in the sunglasses on the table, Alan getting up from the table and making his way briskly out the door.

Brian continues, "I'm just letting you know off the record your boss is squeaky clean. He has a sealed record as a minor that includes arson, but he was a minor."

Seconds later, an argument starts outside the restaurant doors. Alan is arguably upset with a man. Odan's table clears to go outside, excluding Odan and Raymond, who remain at the table.

Miles away at a small airport in California, a sharp-dressed man in his sixties from the Cessna 441 that just landed is now talking to two undercover policemen on the shady side of a large helicopter hangar. The temperature is rising, approaching ninety degrees.

"She's here somewhere and I don't have a clue what she's planning," says Bass to Dag, who has a slight noticeable breathing problem.

"It's not going to end well," the second officer replies. "You guys know that, right?"

"What's our next move? What's in her head? I don't know whether I should be ducking or standing up. In fact, I don't even want to know," the sharp-dressed man states calmly.

"Maybe that's better for me," states Dag, running his left hand through his thinning black hair, blown forward by a shuffling California breeze.

"Who do we call him and what's the connection?" the tall agent asks, as he scans the vicinity, looking for eavesdropping bystanders.

"Call *him*?" the sharp-dressed man says, incredulous. "You stupid asshole, there's no him. The focus is on her. It's like a disease and we need to figure out how much and where to operate to save the patient. Forget about anything you've been told. You're either going to get paid or buried on this one." The gentleman continues, "Does anyone have any idea who the last person she spoke to was when she was inside?" He scans the group slowly.

Looking at his notes on a little pad, the stout officer says, "Dr. Curtis from England . . . Dr. John Collin Curtis to be exact."

"Does anyone get the magnitude of this?" the man in the suit says in a distraught elevated tone. "Does anyone have any idea of what's going to happen if this shit escapes the perimeter? We have to keep this totally off the grid and under control for the next seventy-two hours and find out where she's heading. We need to frame this tight. No one else has to know about this, not even the local authorities. There is no one on the face of this earth that's got survival skills like she does, and I mean period." A small white truck drives through the hangars out onto the tarmac to an awaiting plane. They all pause and gather it in their peripheral.

Looking up, the man in the suit asks, "Who is John Collin Curtis?" A two-minute pause comes over the group. Tension is starting to build as the men become fidgety.

"Dr. Curtis was born in 1966. His father engineered the greatest DNA extraction team in the history of mankind. Rumours were that DNA was placed into capsules at the Hutton Middle School in Bradford, England. The program had a code name, 'Bloodlines.' The school doesn't exist anymore and both Curtis and his father are ghosts in the wind. Today it would be worth billions. It would fuck up the world worse than the plague. It made today's stem cell research look like dollar-store toys."

The tall undercover policeman asks, "What does this have to do with us? Does it have anything to do with our four assists in Vancouver? How the hell did we get chosen for this detail?"

"Those assets were pedophiles that were pulled out of Germany and given new identities," says the man in the suit. If she finds them, they're dead—in fact, they're dead already. As far as she goes . . . she had a tracking device put in her bone marrow when she was sixteen years of age. She got it out, no one knows how. She was impregnated—or if you wanna call it, inseminated—by the government just so they could keep control of the situation and, furthermore, she has your names in her back pocket on a piece of paper. I put it there— if you want to control the flock, you need to control the wolves. She can't get out of frame again. This is just the precipice."

Meanwhile back at the coffee shop, Odan and Raymond are now making their exit and when they get to the front of the restaurant, Alan is confronting a well-groomed man. Getting out of a red-and-white '57 Chevy, the gentleman appears to be eating an apple. Alan approaches the man and his voice can be heard echoing through the restaurant. "I'm gonna drive that piece of fruit down your fucking throat until you choke, you prick!"

Just then, Odan grabs Alan and pulls him back by his right shoulder and says to him, "He's not worth it." The group walk back to their vehicles, discussing something. The gentleman who was in the Chevy walks into the restaurant and tosses his apple core in the garbage.

Trace asks Brian in a quiet voice, "What was that all about?"

Brian replies, "That's Peter Derickson. He's kind of a sleazy businessman who had a run-in with Odan and stabbed him in the back years ago. Rumours were that Peter was, let's just say, having carnal knowledge of a police officer at the station and they tried to take Odan down."

"There's got to be more to that," says Trace with a somewhat confused look on her face as she leans back.

"Are you sure you really want to get into this? It's kinda messed up and he's really, really jaded after all the shit he's had to go through," says Brian.

"It's what I do. It's what I'm good at, and basically just about the only thing I can do, you know," says Trace, as she leans back in her chair. "So what do I have to do to get this story and meet this guy?"

"I'm not getting involved in this," he says. "You've been gone too many years and the only thing I will tell you is he's an inventor, writer and he's got a hangar at the airport where everybody hangs out once in a while. I know I'm probably a little offside, but there's Gwen at Dawn Eva's Greenhouse. You could check that out and I'll just leave it at that. If the rumours are true, this guy's been screwed over more times than anyone I've ever known or heard of, and . . . he's got a shit load of kids," says Brian.

Three minutes go by and Brian says as he stands up to leave, "The girl over in that corner that Derickson is talking to has the hots for Odan." Brian gets up, winks and smiles. He walks cautiously to his vehicle, scanning around, then he jumps in and drives off. Trace sits and waits for a second. Then she gets up and walks out the door and slowly adjusts her head to get a glimpse of the girl and Derickson, flirting at the end of the counter.

Meanwhile, back at the small airport in California, the men are still talking. Agent Bass says, "What's your next move? Where is she going to go?"

The man replies, "She's been locked up for so many years and the only thing I know for certain is there's going to be a big body count."

"What the hell does that mean to us?" asks Dag, as he bends down and grabs a handful of dirt.

"First things first, we need to find out who's on her list and what they mean to us, if anything," the man says.

Agent Dag looks to the other two men. "What has she got for weapons?"

The other two look at each other and the tall one references a file. He closes the file and looks back and says, "She could kill you right now, right where you stand, with a roll of ass wipe and a smile. She's that type of person. No one wants to meet her . . . ever . . . if she's not on your side. She is extremely hot, though—she could double for a model."

"If you need to rub one out, go to the washroom. Right now, I'm concerned about what she knows. Do I make myself clear, agents Dag and Bass?" states the sharp-dressed man in a growly tone, and continues, as he hands Bass a business card. "This is where you start, in Detroit. Take the four-forty-one, then I'll meet you guys out west. I think he's got some unsettled business there."

"I thought we were looking for her, and didn't Hayden just say *he*?" whispers Bass. The sharp-dressed man strides over to the helicopter that awaits him. The helicopter banks a sharp right as it whistles off into the air.

Intel Swell

Trace is driving down the narrow, curvy road into town. Quails scurry across the road in front of her. She cranes her head out the open window, listening to the lyrics of "The Reason." She turns down the volume after the chorus and asks through her Bluetooth, "May I have the number for Dawn Eva's? It's a greenhouse, I believe."

The voice on the other end says, "The number is 777-2121 . . . You will be connected now," and it rings three times.

A young female voice comes on. "Dawn Eva's."

Trace asks, "May I speak to Gwen, please?"

The girl replies, "She's out in the greenhouse. Can I take a message?"

"I'll call back later," says Trace.

The girl replies in a cheery tone, "Sounds good."

"Thank you," Trace says.

Trace drives down a long narrow road. A string of ten Porsches pass her, enjoying the curves. The road now widens and comes into the city, and on the left-hand side past the traffic light is a greenhouse with orange piping outlining the frame. The sign says, "Dawn Eva's." Trace manages to catch the light and turns just in time and pulls into the parking lot. There are a dozen or so cars in the parking lot and the market is bright and open in front. As she's parking her car, her phone goes off. She gazes at the number on the phone but she ignores it because she doesn't recognize it and pushes Mute. The sound of small pebbles bounce off the rocker panels of her car as she comes to a stop. She gets out of her car, straightens her skirt and looks in the side mirror to see whether or not things are in order. Then she proceeds to walk into the greenhouse and as she does, garners up a smile. She's greeted by a tall young girl standing at the cash register, about to serve an elderly lady.

The teenager smiles at Trace and says hello. Trace recognizes the voice from the phone and replies back with a kind voice and asks, "Is Gwen around anywhere?" "She's at the very back by the Italian prune plums," the girl replies.

As Trace walks to the back, the smell of fresh fruit and vegetables is everywhere, suspended in the humidity that kisses the skin. The overhead misters spray the air above her and she slows her gait to enjoy it. She sees a short-haired woman with her back to her; the woman is very curvy and short. The woman turns around, gives her a big smile and asks, "What can I do for ya?"

"I love this place!" Trace says "It's fresh and clean and so colourful. I was told you're the person to ask," Trace begins as she bites her lip.

Gwen shuffles back and forth and replies in a light tone, "Well, I'm standing right here and dying to hear."

"I'm not sure where to start . . . but let's go with this. My name is Trace and I just got here from the Big Apple . . . actually, my family lives here, and I've been assigned to write a story about your friend Odan," says Trace as she backs up a step.

"Well, I hope you get it. That's not a short story or a love story," says Gwen. Then she chuckles and laughs from her belly.

"I'm just trying to get a picture of who he is and who he was and see if there's really a story here," says Trace, frowning, trying to turn it into a smile.

Gwen sighs heavily. "Where do I start? You understand we're talking over twenty years of all kinds of crap—hurt feelings, bad businesses and bad relationships . . . and our families have been in this for some time."

Trying to change the mood, Trace smiles and says, "I think I saw your husband today at the coffee shop. He was with the guys."

"What are you saying? How did you know Alan was my husband?" asks Gwen, moving branches and leaves back to examine some plums.

"A little birdie told me. He was having coffee with Odan, and then they exchanged some pretty vulgar words with a guy named Peter, I believe?" Trace replies. "Holy shit! He didn't try to kill him, did he? So, your brother is a dirty cop," Gwen says with a smirk in her voice as she shuffles backward and grabs some small shovels out of a flower bed.

With a little bit of vibrato in her voice, Trace replies, "He was mad. I heard him make some kind of threat."

"Peter kind of screwed us all over, but mostly Odan. He killed an aircraft company and a water treatment company by opening his big mouth at the wrong time to an executive from the other side," Gwen explains. She takes a step forward and finishes, "Over forty of us took a shit-kicking on that and Odan took the fall. You've been gone a long time. How do you know your brother isn't dirty?"

They both smirk and walk down the aisle together. On arriving at the front, they turn to face each other and Trace states says, "Anything you can tell me would be incredibly appreciated. I just want to get this article started. I'm not looking for anything earth-shattering but if you could give me some sort of insight, it would be a start."

"Well . . . what do you wanna know about cars, music, sports, aviation or women?" Gwen asks Trace, and then she chuckles again.

Back in town, Brian walks through the station door, breezing toward his office. A female officer approaches. "What's new and exciting, Brian?" she asks in a phony happy voice. Her eyes look away from him as he turns to her.

"Nothing that has anything to do with you. If you don't mind me being rude, I have a lot to do and deadlines to meet" He walks past her, down the hallway, and turns right into his office. Her cowardly eyes follow him as he walks away from her. A pursed smile, twisted by glimpses of corruption, is on her face.

A male officer's voice pipes up from his desk halfway down the hall, "Donna, there's a call for you on line two." She walks slowly over to the phone, taking her time. She looks all around before she answers the phone. "Constable Annley," she replies, sitting behind her desk.

The female voice on the other hand says in a firm tone, "You're going down, you crooked bitch!" then hangs up with a heavy click. Constable Annley puts the receiver down and looks out the window with a sense of paranoia.

Back at the greenhouse market, the two women are still talking. "It sounds like there could be a long story here," says Trace.

Gwen smiles and puts her hands on her hips, then a serious look comes over her face. She takes a deep breath and says, "You have to understand. He's a dreamer and an extremely high-energy guy. At least he used to be. Things he took for granted were lost. He let his ego and pride get the best of him. He spent many years with Raymond, for better or worse—and by that, I mean worse. Raymond takes very little mercy in business." There is a long pause as they walk outside into the sunshine. "Odan was torn because he always wanted to be the biggest and the best and didn't want to run over people. Truly, there is no way of knowing where he'd be today if he didn't tell certain people his strategy and dreams." Gwen sighs and smiles, then continues, "Let's talk about the women in his life." She begins to laugh. Without knowing what they're laughing about, Trace joins in.

Gwen continues, "Lynn was way before my time, because Alan and I have only known him about twenty five years. I think he had six kids by four mothers before we even met him. We met him through Raymond years ago. We were going to go into the environmental business. It kind of looked like a home run at first but then things went to shit. Odan is super creative and he's never short of a new idea. Although, in the last ten years, he has slowed down because of what went wrong with his aviation company. He was the CEO of it . . . but there was a crooked shareholder name Peter Derickson." Gwen starts to giggle.

"I thought we were talking about women," says Trace. They both smile and keep talking as they walk through the plants.

In Vancouver, Elon, the attractive, mature lady with the long blond hair strung through the back of a ball cap crosses the street briskly. The door chime goes off as she walks into a women's clothing store. A tall, slim woman in a fitted dress approaches her and says, "Yes, can I help you?"

"I need a few outfits," she replies "One super-casual and one a little dressy, maybe even a little cheesy." She pauses. "Like yours. I'd really like to find out what they're wearing here because I've been out of the game so long. I don't want to stick out like a sore thumb and I'm going to meet family that I haven't seen in a long time."

"Well, I think I can help you there," the sales clerk replies with a contrived smile. A six-foot-plus muscular, tanned man appears from the back. The woman changes her focus and walks toward the man, grinning. She places her gun on the counter. The glass counter scratches like fingernails on a chalkboard. As she walks past him, his face darkens with the knowledge that she's there for him. He pulls out a .44 Magnum from behind his back. Deep, thick shots ring out as he fires the gun three times. She lunges toward him and blocks his wrist. The gun goes flying through the air, bouncing off and shattering a seven-foot glass mirror and resting on the floor. They exchange twenty short-range blows in what seems like a split second. He grabs her by the throat with his right hand and throws her over a shoe rack and she tumbles. Shoes and shirts fall like dominoes on the hard tile floor. She doesn't make a sound, not a growl or grunt, almost machine-like. Then she stands up and gives both the man and woman a blank, cold stare. She straightens herself out and walk slowly around the rack. He smiles as a small trace of blood appears over her left eye and walks up to her thinking he's in control. She reaches out with her right foot and kicks him in the throat, knocking him on his back and head against a coat rack five feet from the resting gun. They stare at each other as she walks toward him. He breathes heavily as she gets close. Her right arm brushes against the clothes on the rack and makes a little jingle.

She whispers gently, her face not more than four inches apart from his, "Are you going to fight this?"

He tries to speak but only gets two words out: "Tour Guide."

She pulls out a knife and stabs him quickly five times in the chest. "Yes, I am. Your passport has been revoked," she says quietly. She reaches down into his pants pocket and pulls out a lanyard then she stands and turns. The woman is facing her, holding the gun pointed at her. She walks toward her as the clock on the wall goes *tick . . . tick . . . tick*. She quickly grabs some black plimsolls from the shoe rack, and whirls them through the air, knocking the gun out of her hand.

Distraught, the woman says, "Who are you? What do you want from me?" as she attempts to hold back tears.

"I'm here as a guardian angel sent to right wrongs. You can call me arma, Jane or just another bitch that forgot to take her holy basil. I'm here to kill you on behalf of the sixty children you and your associates raped over nine days in Hanover, Germany." She knees the woman in the chest and she falls to the floor gasping and grunting in front of her. She starts whimpering as the woman standing over her slowly removes her knife from its sheath.

The Tour Guide says to her, "You can't fight the tears that aren't coming." She grabs the woman's hair with her left hand and stabs her in the neck and twists and says in an eerie, soft German tone, "One less *schmutzig . . . loch.*" She gets up and cleans the blade of the knife with the girl's hair. Slowly, she retrieves her gun. She walks toward the door and says out loud, "I'm trying to remember if I did take my holy basil today."

The two agents walk into the office of the female attorney in Detroit. Casually, but with purpose. The door doesn't even have a chance to close before the attorney starts talking, "She was here and I mean she was *just here.* Standing right where you guys are standing right now."

The shorter agent states, "I'm Agent Phil Dag, and my colleague here is Agent Bass. Now, tell us what the hell happened, Janice."

"She got out and wants to play?" Janice replies quickly in an elevated tone. "You guys were supposed to have that shit under control and now I got a psychological weapon out there that should've been put down decades ago. Hold your tampons and I hope you're done, because it's not only me she wants to fuck over. She's out for some payback . . . and give me the only reason she's doing this shit after over thirty years. Oh, that's right, you cocksuckers had her locked up at our company's expense!"

Bass walks toward the window behind the lawyer's desk. "Face it. The only reason we are all still above the dirt is because she wants us to be above the dirt. Let's revamp our lines of communication and keep some of this crap off the grid. We need to find out what she's up to. We have to make sure we take care and clean this up—and fast," he says.

"Does she even know who she is? She's had so much shit in her system over the years," says Janice. She gets up and adjusts her jacket.

"So far the damage is minimal, but then again we have no idea what collateral damage she planning," says Bass.

Janice blows a sarcastic kiss from across the office. "That's me kissing your ass because I want this over with. That's as close as you're going to get, and by the way, behind you on that chair—that box—that box is a present and this fucking time it isn't for me." Her cell rings.

Trace and Gwen are seated at a picnic table at the edge of the market in front of the greenhouse. It's hot and dry outside. You can hear the faint sound of the irrigation system. Baby quail are running through the open area between the long narrow orange stands of peaches and cucumbers, and an ever-so-slight breeze is coming from the south over the lake. Trace puts her sunglasses on.

Gwen places both her hands on the table and clasps them together firmly. "Well, where were we?" she asks.

"I think we were talking about women," replies Trace.

Gwen looks down then up with a little smile. "He's got a diary. It's like the holy grail. He keeps his work in there . . . his inventions. We've joked about it over the years even though we've never seen him write in it, but we have seen him close it up. Al threatened once that he was going to get it photocopied. The look he was given was not an impressed one."

"Any clue what else is in it"? Trace asks.

"Everything . . . maybe nothing. No, I probably shouldn't say that, because I know damn well there's dirty secrets in there," Gwen says. There's a moment of silence as they both look at each other and smile. There's a soothing sound of vehicles in the background, driving past the greenhouse. Another soft breeze blows through, bringing the smell of the orchards into the market. A tour bus pulls up and a dozen or so Asians of all ages start wandering into the market.

Over the public address system, a woman's voice says, "Gwen, can you please come to the front?"

"Walk with me," Gwen says. They get up from the table and start walking back to the greenhouse. Trace notices that the faster she goes, Gwen walks with a noticeable limp, favouring her left side. Trace browses the plants while Gwen serves customers. Eventually, Gwen comes over. "I think we're good now. Do you still want to talk?"

"I would love that," Trace says and they head back outside.

"He wrote something years ago," Gwen says. "It was planned as a joke—or maybe not—when he was in a relationship spin."

Trace sits up and asks, "Am I going to laugh?"

"You can't use it, but it was kind of funny at the time. It was almost like something you'd see on a dating website," Gwen says.

"I promise I won't write anything that would hurt him," Trace says. "So tell me about this funny bit of writing that you were talking about."

Gwen takes a deep breath and says, "Well, it's just funny but I'm afraid it will give you the wrong impression of him." And then, with her country smile, she says, "I still have a crinkled copy of it."

"I promise it can be off the record," Trace says again in a softer tone, but Gwen stands up. She straightens out her smock and tilts her head a little bit.

"You seem to be a nice girl, but I hope you understand I'm in a little bit of a spot."

"I'm just looking for some interesting anecdotes that won't hurt anybody," Trace says attempting to come across as the girl next door to win Gwen over.

Gwen gives her a subtle look up and down and says, "You're probably his kind and he probably would talk to you, but you can't go hard and heavy with this story." She starts walking away, then turns and looks over her left shoulder. "Are you buying lunch today? Because I'm off in forty-five."

Smiling, Trace puts her hand on her right hip and says, "Just tell me where, girl."

ZZ Top's "La Grange" plays on the stereo as the black Ford truck with the inch-and-a-quarter raised aluminum letters spelling "Stepchild" on the back of the box comes over the hill at sixty miles an hour. The vibrato sound of exhaust caroms off the hill. The driver's cell phone rings and he pushes Connect on the screen. "Odan here," he answers.

"How's the bed-wetter?" asks Kelly.

"How are you doing, Kelly?" Odan replies.

"Are you buying the Budweiser?" asks Kelly.

"Are you buying the steak?" Odan flings back.

"It's your restaurant. Why the hell would I do something like that?" Kelly laughs. "Does two o'clock sound good?" Odan asks.

"Thought you were working on that little thing up on Rich," Kelly says.

Just then, Odan looks back over his shoulder into the box of his truck and notices a toolbox and a can of transmission fluid. He says, "Kelly, did you leave your toolbox and oil in the back of my truck?" Four seconds go by and he says it again, "Kelly, are you still there or did I lose you?"

"Yeah I'm here. I forgot it. I was up at your house on Wednesday. In fact, I forgot where I left it. I'll pick it up at Bud time."

"Not a problem," replies Odan.

Kelly ends the call and stands up. The construction site is overrun with a bunch of bean counters gazing past the house, looking down at a small patch of land with a Bailey bridge barely four feet wide leading to a little cabin made of stone and cedar. He says, "I've got an appointment, guys. I'll be back in a bit." The gentlemen say nothing and he walks over to the side of the road where his red SUV is parked.

The mysterious Tour Guide has pulled into the small town of Candid, set between two mountain ridges near Mason. She is now sporting a new set of clothes. She wears blue jeans, a pair of Nike runners and a green windbreaker. She places her sunglasses on top of her head and looks up to the right as a small plane passes over. Then she walks toward a pewter Flex parked on the side of the road between the convenience store and the gas station. She stops by the Flex door. She knows something is askew, and she purposely drops her keys. She bends over to grab her keys and casually checks underneath the van. She gets up, shrugs, and goes to the other side of the vehicle. As she approaches the bumper, she pulls her cell phone out of her pocket and sticks it to the van, as it is magnetized. The cell phone quickly dials a predetermined number and on the other end of the line a male voice answers, "Hello."

The Tour Guide stands still and replies, "Don't miss."

On the crest of the hill opposite the town, two men stand by a vehicle; the older man with a pair of binoculars and the younger one with a high-powered rifle. Just as the man raises the rifle and looks through the scope, a twenty-two-inch arrow pierces his throat and he drops to the ground. The one with the binoculars has a cell phone in his hand and just as his phone rings, he drops to his knee and looks around. It's very quiet. The only sound is the hum of the small town below. There is nothing visible behind him. The Tour Guide goes quickly around to the front of the Flex, opens it, stops for a second, looks up at the side of the hill and smiles. She gets in and slowly drives away from the curb. She takes her sunglasses off and places them on the dashboard then she talks into a cell phone on her Bluetooth and abruptly says, "Kite." After eight rings the phone is answered.

On the other end, Janice says, "Why are you doing this?

"You know why I'm doing this. You know I can't take my foot off the throttle now. Your fuck-ups, your front door. I'm the Reaper. I gave you a chance to clean your mess many years ago, but you're so dirty I'm surprised your tits haven't rotted off. Next time I see you I'm going to alter the whites in your eyes. Bye for now, bitch."

There is a *click* as she ends the call.

Nestled on the ridge a mile from the lake is a quaint little restaurant with great views of the valley. It used to be named The Minstrel and is now called The Lizard and Chicken. It is off the beaten path but still in Mason. Trace is sitting at a booth. The investigative reporter in her can't help but take notes in her mind of her surroundings. Music is playing at the perfect volume for her mind, keeping her heart and thoughts aligned. The seats are dark brown. The backs are burgundy with rust piping. The surroundings are quaint and inviting. She notices a Rob Thomas song playing in the background. The solid cedar tables are completed with teal napkins and heavy black silverware. The bifold doors are open. You can hear the muted sound of traffic as well as the trickle of a small brook that is only thirty feet away. The edge of the property overlooks a crack in the warm cedar fence. Small plants adorn the fence where a board is missing

Trace runs her hands along the top of the cedar table and looks back up, rolls a pen in her right hand. She looks out the window as cyclists pass by. The music changes to one of her favourite songs, "Stand By Me." A server in a soft summer dress comes up and says, "My name is Channi. Can I get you anything?"

Channi is always smiling. She is a gorgeous, tall brunette with shoulder-length hair and a small mole on her neck where it meets her collarbone.

"What are the specials?" Trace asks, smiling back.

"We don't have any specials today because we're going to be switching over to a new menu soon. But everything is fantastic here. The owner swears by the double gin martini."

"That sounds good. I haven't had one of those in a while."

"It's Odan's favourite," Channi says.

"Did I hear you say Odan?" Trace asks in an intrigued tone.

Channi politely smiles and says, "Yes, he's the owner," then she walks away. Channi feels Trace's eyes on her as she departs and she smiles to herself.

Trace looks out the perfectly cleaned window as an orange Land Rover convertible pulls in, parking beside a black Ducati Monster motorcycle. Gwen steps out of her vehicle, looks down at her seat and grabs a small green bag. She walks with a smile, takes four strides and stops, then looks up as if she's forgotten something. She turns around and goes back to her vehicle. She leans over the door and grabs a piece of paper out of the backseat. She looks up and smiles as she notices Trace in the window of the restaurant.

The Old World paving stones and rocks leading up to the nine-foot oak doors are arranged in a charming diagonal pattern. The restaurant is made of tall timbers, modern glass and tasteful stone. As Gwen walks through the entrance, she notes Lizzie, the GM, in the back, and the young lady two tables down from where Trace is sitting. There is a subtle aviation theme to the decor with several brass model airplanes hung from the ceiling. Gwen takes a seat on the bench by the window across from Trace, facing her.

As she sits down, Trace asks, "Gwen, why do they call this place 'The Lizard and Chicken'?"

Gwen replies, "You have to ask Odan. He's changing it soon to the 'The Wet Spot'"

"I will if I ever get a chance to meet him," Trace answers, grinning inside at the new name Gwen told her.

Gwen takes her cell phone with her left hand and brings it under the table and starts sending a text as she continues to talk. "Oh, I'm sure that that could probably happen, depending on how you play your cards. As long as you keep the jokers up your sleeve." Gwen now places her orange cell phone that matches her car on the table face up.

Trace says casually, glancing up at the speaker above Gwen's head, "This is one of my favourite songs. I'm kind of a music buff."

Gwen smiles. "How was your drive? I take it you found this place just fine?" She picks up her fork and knife and stands them up like little marching soldiers then sets them down again.

Channi returns to the table with Trace's martini and asks Gwen, "What can I get you for a drink?"

"Should I dare try a double gin and tonic?" she asks Trace with a smile, then turns back to Channi. "Sure, why not? I can call Al to come pick me up or even use Uber. I've called Al for worse."

Three separate groups of people arrive at the restaurant. The last is a couple in their fifties. They're holding hands.

Gwen sits back in her seat and says, "It won't be long now."

Trace has a puzzled look on her face and asks, "What do you mean, it won't be long now?"

"It's Friday. Odan's friends and family will be here shortly," Gwen announces. "Why couldn't you have told me this at the greenhouse?" Trace asks.

"I wanted to know a little bit about you and what you're up to first. Let's just call it a feeling-out-process," states Gwen.

Back at Janice's office in Detroit, Janice answers the phone. She has been taking notes in a very heavy two-tone ledger. She pushes the Speaker button. The male voice on the other end says in a very deflated tone, "We missed."

"What happened?" Janice asks, as she leans back in her chair.

The voice says, "We had her . . . just couldn't close, and we lost our best shooter." A puzzled angry look comes over Janice's face. She throws a blue Matryoshka doll across the room and it smashes in a thousand pieces.

"Just walk up to the bitch and stab her in the back!" Janice's tone approaches shouting.

"She knew we were coming," the male voice states, creeping toward a hoarse whisper. Continuing, he says, "If it was that easy, why didn't you do it yourself when you had her in your office two days ago?"

"The next time you get this close to her, it will either be in a dream or you're dead. Have you read all the files?" she asks.

"I don't want to be within one hundred miles of this creature, let alone try to stab this thing in the back. I'm not quite sure how, but we need to figure this shit out and we need to figure it out right now. Do we have any clue where she's going or what she's up to?" the male voice questions.

Janice replies, "Sorry, un-fuckin'-fortunately not . . . it's a 'need to know' file." She slams down the phone and turns it off. Then she whispers to herself, "And to think she used to be my best friend."

Warm air blows into The Lizard and Chicken as the door is opened, and friendly Channi walks by and drops off Gwen's drink.

"Are you ladies ready to order?" Channi smiles.

Trace says, "We're going to have a couple of your Kickin' Prime and Shrimp on page three."

Gwen states, "That's soooo cool! I never had that before."

Channi replies after a shrug of her nose, "Kickin' Prime and Shrimp comin' right up."

"So, where were we?" says Trace.

Gwen reaches out with her right hand and touches Channi gently on the side before she leaves. "Are you the same girl that . . .?

"Oh, yes," Channi replies. "Yes, I cut off your husband," she says with a smile. Then she walks away with a cute little grin and a quick gait. Gwen leans over the table puts the straw in her mouth and has a big sip, just like a schoolgirl. "Ahh, yeah," she says. "This is sure good." She straightens and looks curiously at Trace. "So tell me. You're a big city girl? What brings you here?"

A slight breeze flows through the aisle of the restaurant as the door is opened again. The tablecloth of the big round table nearest the door does a slight wave. Trace looks over and it's the only table that has Reserved marked on it. In walks a very heavyset three-hundred-pound redheaded man with a red beard dressed in a grey T-shirt, light blue shorts and sandals. He is talking to someone walking behind him, catching up. Behind him is a woman approximately twenty years his senior with glasses and a smock shirt, and a man dressed very casually. The manager seats them at a table on the opposite side of the restaurant to Trace's far left. Both women gaze out the window as the parking lot starts to fill up. A white Ford Taurus SHO and a yellow VW Beetle pull into the lot and park beside each other. The pair of couples are talking about something while they're still seated in their cars with the windows rolled down. Then they all get out and walk toward the door, smiling and laughing. One of the girls waves through the window at Gwen. Gwen holds her hand up and gestures back.

As they walk through the door toward the big round table marked Reserved, Trace says, "Who are those people?"

"Odan's people," Gwen replies.

"What do you mean, his people?" she asks.

"The tall one is his son, and the girl I waved at is his daughter. In fact, that large redheaded man over on the bench on the far side is with his mother and stepfather. He is also Odan's son, Leif."

"You mean the overweight guy?" she says.

"No," Gwen says. "I said large and meant fat."

"The tall one is Jon, and the girl I waved at is Stephanie. His boys are known to have a little attitude and be a little hotheaded, except 'Man-cub' and Odan's daughter Stephanie . . . let's just call her 'D-plus' when it comes to smarts."

"Which one is Man-cub?" Trace asks.

"Man-cub is Odan's youngest son," Gwen says. She pauses to take a sip of her cocktail. "This is the one night they all get together. His three sons are all from different mothers . . . yeah, you heard me. I'm not sure, but they have to be over eight years apart from top to bottom. I have something I want to give you, Trace, but I need permission from him to give it to you."

Trace cocks her head with uninhibited curiosity.

Five miles away from the restaurant, Odan's cell rings inside of his truck. He answers. "Hello, can I help you?" The voice on the other end is a woman. Quite apparently she's drunk.

"I'll always love you," says the voice.

"Yeah, right," he says with a smirk. "Esme, it's good to hear from you."

"Have you heard from Man-cub?" she slurs and continues. "Man-cub says he's going to move and spend more time with you."

Odan steps on the gas as he rounds the corner and his truck goes a little sideways. He says, "I got to go. I've got another line blazing in here. Can we talk a little later?"

"I wanna talk to you right now," she says.

He replies, "It will have to be after eight because we're having a shindig. I'm pulling up now." He hits a cellular dead zone as he comes around the corner.

Jon, Odan's middle son, is six foot two, one-hundred-and-eighty pounds, with short brown hair, brown eyes and a beard. He's wearing a designer black Mandarin shirt, jeans and tan dress shoes. He gets up from his seat and walks toward the girls, waving with a shit-eating grin. When he's two feet away he says in a cheerful tone, "How are you doing, Gwen?"

Gwen moves over and Jon settles beside her then asks, "So, what brings you out?"

She replies, "The answers to both your questions are right in front of you. This is Trace." Both Jon and Trace extend their hands to shake gently.

He looks up at her and says to Trace, "You don't work at a greenhouse with hands like that, and—by the way— it's nice to meet you."

He looks down at his cell phone and it shows a text message from Stephanie, his sister. He doesn't read it but quickly voice-texts her back, "You're a dill hole," then puts the cell back in his pocket.

"Trace is doing an article on your father," says Gwen.

Jon stands up and says, "Well, very nice to meet you, enjoy." He looks at Gwen and adds, "I don't trust her."

He gives a little bow, and as he starts to walk away, Trace says, "Why? You don't know me."

He leans over to her and whispers, "You have no idea how many females have screwed over my dad." A big smile comes over his face, then he straightens, turns and casually walks back to his table.

"I'm sorry. I should've warned you about him," says Gwen.

"Oh, there's no problem. I would expect nothing less from somebody trying to protect his dad. And after all, he is his father's son, is he not?" Trace states with her knowing smile.

"Yes, he is, but he's nothing compared to Odan," Gwen says.

Channi brings by another cocktail and the girls are almost finished their meal. The music in the restaurant is slowly gaining in volume. "I Want to Break Free" now plays.

"I love this song, too," Trace says wistfully, moving her head to the song's intro. Then she hears someone in the restaurant say, "He's here," and in walks Odan: six foot one, two-hundred-and-ten pounds, chiselled, blue-eyed and handsome, tight beard, forty-five years old, dressed in a deep-blue sports jacket and black T-shirt with burgundy writing on it that says "Playing with a Broken Moon," designer jeans and new white DC runners. He walks toward the round table and just as he's about to sit down, his son Jon gives a hand signal with a nod to Odan to look over at Gwen's table. Odan glances over and decides to come pay a visit. As he approaches the table, it's apparent he has something on his mind.

"This is the young lady I've been hearing all about, correct?" he stated, with no introduction.

Trace replies before Gwen has an opportunity to talk. "Yes, my name is Trace Scott and I'm putting together a story on you. That is, of course, if you'll let me."

He pulls back his jacket and puts his hands in his pockets, then leans in Trace's direction. "You look like a fine girl—in fact, you're borderline hot—but you have to understand the answer you'll get from me is a simple no. It doesn't take that long in these times to figure out who are the parasites and who are the weak and how the puzzle fits. I could be wrong. Your intentions could be one-hundred-percent pure, but I still don't see how that does me any good after all these years and everything I've had to go through. There is no story here. It's simple. I'm just a washed-up dreamer that's been screwed over so many times the whorehouses went out of business. I bet that the little prick down at the paper—Gary, driving that fancy Bentley—said you could have a job if you could find out more about me, yeah?"

Reluctantly, Trace replies, "You're right. He did offer me a job, but as I started digging into this, I realized something here is a little bit off and it's intriguing the shit out of me."

Odan plunks himself down on an empty chair and says, "I'll tell you what. I'll give you an inch on this one and then after that I'll have to cut you free. Day after tomorrow, nine o'clock at my office, if you got it in ya. Excuse me, I have to get back to my family and friends and have a little fun. Once again, Trace, it was very nice to meet you. Gwen, cover your ass with both hands . . . this one could be wild."

On his way back to the table, he first stops and talks to Channi and says, "Make sure the girls have at least a titch on the table at all times."

Just then a man walks in. Odan turns to his right and meets him halfway to the door and says, "Hey, Kel, you made it, buddy." And then they both proceed through the crowd toward the big round table and Odan says to Channi, "Please get Kelly a Seizure—that's a triple Caesar."

When Channi is out of earshot, Kelly says, "What's up with that girl? Ya think she can't wipe her ass without music like you? She's hot!"

"Which one?" Odan asks

"Your server," says Kelly.

"I thought you were talking about that number over at the table sitting with Gwen," Odan says.

"Oh, now that I notice, should we be buying her a drink?" Kelly asks.

"Just trying to take care of my new friend," says Odan in a non-condescending tone. They both sit down at the same time and Odan pushes the menu away. He continues, "Now that I think about it, why should I buy her a drink? I don't know what she's up to, number one . . . and number two, I'm not interested in any."

Odan rubs his chin and is about to talk when Kelly interrupts, "How long has it been? Or are you just a chicken?"

"I might be a chicken, but you're a dog, Kelly." They both laugh.

"Well, at least I'm gettin' some." Kelly chuckles.

"I could get some. I'm just focused right now and I don't want any more drama," says Odan.

He takes a sip of his martini that has been sitting, waiting for him. Kelly giggles, smirks and stirs his Seizure with the celery and says, "You're gettin' old."

Back at Gwen's table, the mood has subdued a little. Trace tries to break the silence. "It could've gone a lot worse," she says with a smile. "He could've shot me." Gwen nods with a grin. She pulls a piece of paper off the seat and says, "This is a good one. Please use it wisely."

"What is this?" Trace asks, as she uncrinkles a four-page letter that has a coffee stain three quarters up on it.

"Years ago, the big guy was joking around after having a cocktail and put this together to scare off any would-be suitors. He had intentions of putting it on a dating website. I'm gonna catch a lot of shit for this one. Don't you dare read it in here. Just let's enjoy ourselves."

Over the next two hours, Odan sends a few drinks to the ladies' table—triples, all. Conversations and laughter continue. Trace looks up and Odan is gone. Trace and Gwen finish with small talk of kids and Al. They get in their cars against better judgment and they leave their separate ways.

Trace looks down at the piece of paper on the passenger seat and picks it up and puts it back down again. She turns on her stereo and there's an Ed Sheeran song on the radio. She drives home staring off into space and wondering what is in that letter that could be of any significance to her. A warm shiver goes through her. She pulls up to her childhood home that she knows so well. The kitchen light is still on. She sees her brother and father through the window, sitting and talking. The lights go off in her car and she looks down at that piece of paper and grabs it and roll it into a tube. It's a beautiful night as she walks to the house from the car. The breeze from the orchards rekindle feelings of nostalgia. The breeze is only strong enough to move one side of the swing that sits on the veranda and the dog trots gently behind her, carrying a tennis ball in its mouth.

She opens both doors and walks in and her brother and father turn to greet her. The men say nothing else as Trace walks toward the kitchen, dropping her jacket on the chair to her right. She pulls out a dining chair and the wood scratches against the floor. Then she bites her lip as she slowly unravels the crumpled tube of paper that was given to her from Gwen. Her brother says with his back turned a few feet from her, "Be careful, sis."

She reads the letter, mumbling, barely out loud, not loud enough to be heard. Her father turns and says, "What is it?"

"I can't decide. He's either an asshole or a genius," Trace states.

"You met Odan," says her father as he walks toward her.

With a subtle groan her brother says, "Leave it alone, Trace."

"It's hard," she says. "He gives off this two-sided Dr. Jekyll and Dr. Hyde kind of personality."

"You mean Dr. Jekyll and Mr. Hyde," says her dad.

"No," she says, smirking. "What I meant is they're both smart. Maybe just one is a smart ass."

Trace tells the guys that she's going to bed. As she's climbing the staircase, her brother says, "He's a nice-enough guy, but can't you do something else? Isn't there anything else you can do? Maybe just work on a farm somewhere?"

She stops and says, "Yeah, and you can go suck farts out of bus seats. Is there any chance that this is going to involve you at all, Brian? Did you see anything by any chance? Because I need to know if there's a way that this is all going to come back on me somehow."

She takes two more steps up the stairs and her father says, "Do what your heart says, hon."

Brian says sarcastically, "Let it lead you somewhere you can't get back from." "You guys are messed up. It has nothing to do with that. This is strictly business. But I do admit he intrigues me. Who are you to say what I do? This is who I am."

She goes to her room and closes her door. She's focused on the four pieces of paper and can't take her eyes off of them. She undresses and switches hands holding the paper. It seems like every third sentence, she has to back up and reread it again because it seems so unreal. Could this be him? Could this be all that it is? Is this the right time, or is this a train wreck about to happen?

Now in bed, she stretches and grabs a T-shirt from her dresser and puts it in bed beside her. She places the paper face up on the T-shirt and closes her eyes. Her thoughts can't change what has already happened. She has totally memorized every word on those pages.

The moon stares at the words through the window and Trace eventually falls asleep, recording every word on the pages for a dreamed rehearsal. The morning comes. A breeze blows through the open window and it is as if she never stopped reading the letter. She spends the whole morning walking in the orchard with a notepad and her cell phone.

It's two o'clock in the afternoon. Trace makes an important phone call. The receptionist on the other end answers, "Pillar and Post."

"Is Grayson in? Can I speak with him?" she asks.

"Absolutely! Trace, how are you?"

"I'm fine," she states.

"Are you enjoying the West Coast?" the receptionist asks.

"So far so good. How are things there?" Trace asks.

"Things are good here. I'll put you through."

"I was wondering when I was going to hear from you," the male voice on the other end says with a slight growl. "How are you doing?"

"I'm doing okay. I need a favour from you," Trace says.

"What's it going to cost me?" he asks.

She bites her lip and says, "I'm just doing a little research. I'm going to email you the details right now."

"I'm curious. You never ask anybody for anything. Why now?" he questions.

"This is important to me. I'd be happy if you can find out anything. Now, I've got to turn this phone off and go for a swim," she says.

"You're babbling and rambling on. Take care of yourself. I'll take care of this for you," he says.

"Thank you," she says and turns her phone off and puts it in her pocket.

The man on the other end of the phone was Mr. Grayson Post. He now sits, pondering for a moment, in his large corner office at the newspaper. He clicks on his incoming email, and sees a message from Trace. He pushes a button on his phone and it rings four times on the other end. It's answered by woman with a strong British accent.

"Hello . . . we need to find a couple of parents and reunite the family," he says. The British voice on the other end says, "Send me the info and I'll get on the wire to the agency in an hour."

"Thanks," he replies and reaches over and ends the call.

5

The Big Meet

It's six o'clock in the morning and the weather can't make up its mind in Coldstream. The little drizzle of rain comes down when the clouds drift overtop, and then the sun breaks through and this is how it goes, back and forth. Trace is torn between putting her hair in a ponytail or leaving it down. As she looks in the mirror and turns her head sideways she finally decides that she's going to leave her hair down. She grabs the letter off the end table and her blue Hootie and the Blowfish hoodie off the back of the chair and heads down the stairs. She glances to her left and notices both her mom and dad are having a coffee in the kitchen. She waves and says, "I've got to go."

Her dad asks, "Are you going to meet him today?"

She slows down her gait to stop at the door, then turns her head to look at him and says with a quiet stare, "I think so, if all goes well."

She proceeds out the door, lucky to catch a small window where the sun is shining and there is no drizzle. She climbs into her car and backs it up as she turns on the intermittent wipers, and then turns them off again.

She drives to the coffee shop where she first saw Odan, parks and turns off her car, then makes her way into the restaurant with a deliberate stride. Right away, she sees the man Odan was with yesterday; Gwen said his name was Kelly. He's sitting to her right. He has that strong, handsome wolverine look to him. She pretends not to see him and goes to the far left of the diner where she sits down and spreads the papers in front of her on the table and pushes them a short distance in front of her to ensure she doesn't spill any coffee on them. The letter is not dated. She begins to read it again.

Hello, it's me Odan. It's important to know who I am. I believe I am a high-energy, eclectic, spontaneous, independent, entrepreneurial, confident, witty, quixotic, compassionate, funny and caring man. Wow! What a mouthful. My head is swelling just dictating this. There are very few grey zones in my life. I live life to its max. I sleep less than 45 hours a week. For the most part, the spark in my life is gone. I am a morning person. I like to make my bed before 7:30 AM Pacific Time, unless I'm under the weather. I rarely use alarm clocks and never hit the snooze button. I turn it off and get up. I normally go to bed between 11 PM and midnight. I never pack the day I am leaving. I always pack the day before. I believe it isn't how many breaths you take, but what takes your breath away. I am with fault. I have made changes in my life to be a better man and will always continue to do so. I respect the opinions of others and try to grow within them. I respect the beliefs of individuals. I have a lot

of pet peeves, which I have noted here. Here are some simple truths about me:

I am adopted and have never met my biological parents. The parents who raised me loved me and I love them but I can honestly say I'm sure that if you had asked them what my best subject in school was, what my favourite food was, they would have had no idea. If you asked them what position I played in any sport, they would have said they don't know because they never attended a game. My parents were busy working to put food on the table but I never had an opportunity to throw a ball or anything of the sort with either one of my parents, and that's my biggest regret.

Here are the stats. Baseball: I was a pitcher. #56 (fast and wild). Hockey: I played centre and defence, but my last year I was as a goalie. #22, #11, #35. Football: I was a punter and running back. #1, #22. Stock car racing: #00, #87, #56.

My favourite colours are blue, maroon and white. I hate when assholes try to tell me white is not a colour . . . then why the hell can I buy it in a paint? There will never be a fridge magnet or any other shit on my fridge . . . take the average IQ and deduct 5 pts for every magnet on the fridge and that's the intelligence of the home owner. I don't wear . . . and no one should . . . mismatched socks or socks with holes in them. I can't stand it when I grab a refrigerator or stove door and there is crusty food left on the handle.

I can't stand those lazy fuckin' parasites in their 50s who've got a bunch of children that they don't take care of, and they think that they're God's gift to mankind, and they're just hanging around waiting for one of their parents to die to get their inheritance. I can't stand their hypocritical, "Why me?" pity-party bullshit. They usually have a couple of children from a couple of different relationships, living in a different town or even a different state. You'll find them driving their girlfriend's/boyfriend's car that they met on a dating website.

My old friend Orland once told me that no friend would ever sue another friend and if they did, they weren't a friend to begin with. I can't understand left-wing jerks who tell me what I can or can't say or how to discipline my own children. I do not procrastinate and expect the same from my lady. When I see a man on the street with a wrinkly shirt, I assume he's not in a relationship or has a lazy wife. I never want to be that man. I want to share my highs and lows with my partner in life.

I am very neat and organized and always will be that way. I enjoy cooking and always will contribute when it comes to cleaning. Clothes (especially clean ones) don't need to take up permanent residence on the floor or in laundry baskets. I don't believe in wasting food, so it is important to note I get upset when food is thrown in the garbage. I am not a couch potato. I won't have blankets on my couch because they belong on the bed, but I appreciate downtime to relax.

I TRY to explain all my expectations at the beginning of a relationship. I believe one of the key elements in a successful relationship is communication. To me, eye contact is very important, if not crucial. The key to a relationship's demise or failure is unmet expectations. Don't try to do something or be someone you are not. I will continue trying to improve as a person and role model for my sons, daughters and grandchildren.

Children who require more than one opportunity to be rehabilitated from recreational drug abuse should be sterilized. Adult children who continue to have drug abuse issues should be ignored until such a time that they pass acceptable testing. Should my adult children decide that they no longer need me in their lives, I will accept that.

Don't do things in the beginning of the relationship that you have no interest in, aptitude for or intent of doing in the future. It's true a man can decide when there is to be intimacy and not. I won't beg for physical attention like a puppy at the dining room table looking for scraps.

I won't have a doily in my home because I believe Grandma was eaten by the Big Bad Wolf. Is it too much to ask that my closet be colour-coordinated? With all of my shirts on the same rack?

Don't wear a ball cap in my home because no ball will be played there. I don't sit around and read warm, fuzzy books. Video games shouldn't regularly consume you (more than 4 hrs a week), but there are exceptions to every rule. I dislike any killing video games. Killing video games will not be on my property. I exercise 4 days a week: Monday, Tuesday, Thursday and Friday . I vacuum on Wednesdays and dust on a day thereafter.

I don't trust women who turn their cell phones over when I enter the room or when we are alone. I must cohabitate with a woman for 90 days in a Canadian winter to determine whether or not she will have access to the thermostat. My woman must have the ability to prepare and consume 28 consecutive meals at home without eating out. I'd rather be getting busy with a 6.85, than shut out by a 10. I don't believe in associating with exes or exes' families unless there are children from the relationship.

I have been known to talk with my hands, so don't be surprised if you see me use them. There are religious beliefs I find hypocritical and full of nepotism. In the future, I will never again live in a house that I don't own or have a financial interest in or contribute to. I won't walk around on pins and needles waiting for those famous words, "If you don't like it, leave." The middle finger is not in my gesture handbook. A quiet storm may be brewing if I'm rubbing my right earlobe. Did I mention I'm funny? I don't want a woman who is so sensitive that I have to hang on her every word and edit everything I say. I am me.

I'm looking for someone who is: passionate, independent, spontaneous, sensual, intelligent, funny, humble, confident, caring, honest and respectful. I am looking for a woman who is attractive and who will be at least 66 when I am 100 years of age(although I will never reach it). And she needs to be between 1.5 meters to 1.82 metres in height. A woman who is 1.53 tall or less should not weigh more than 55 kg. I'm looking for someone who doesn't want to be surgically enhanced unless it's necessary. I like it when the carpet matches the drapes, but I especially like it when there is no carpet. I prefer a woman who has a smaller waist than chest. She can't have hobbit or troll feet. Take care of your feet. I don't want a woman who shaves her legs in my bath water. A woman who has junk in the trunk she can move is intoxicating.

I am not an ottoman and don't consider putting your feet on me as cuddling. I will drive as much as possible; I have been in too many accidents with women behind the wheel. I am not much of a perfume or cologne man and believe that makeup is to be used to bring out a woman's highlights not to be applied like Polyfilla. A little attitude in a woman is more than acceptable; in fact, it is a requirement. I want someone with a little spunk. If you're a woman who has an issue with gas, take something for it, A Dutch oven is such a boner killer. I am looking for that one magical person who shares my belief in physical and mental fitness. I don't want a woman who is fickle or fussy. I want someone who knows what she wants. I have a love for children and would accept my woman's children as my own should she have them already. Her children would not receive special treatment and should they use any narcotics that I don't believe in, they would not be acknowledged. Should my authority ever be undermined in matters of discipline, the relationship will be terminated. I want a woman who believes our personal, financial and intimate affairs are private and not to be shared with others.

The problem I have is that mature women are set in their ways, good or bad. Young women, on the other hand, are just that: some are immature and some are know-it-alls . . . bullies. These women are easy to pick out in a crowd. The conversation always has to revolve around them and it has to be about their subject knowledge. They will correct you at every opportunity and cut your sentences off midstream. They think they are always right. These women rarely change, so I run from them; I already have one in the family like this.

The lack of respect I have received in previous relationships has left me somewhat jaded, but has brought my own faults to the surface. Lululemon may have been invented by God himself. I am right-handed, but I've been known to do a small load of laundry with either. Paying attention to detail is important. I don't have any allergies that I know of, other than drama and whining. If you are allergic to beef, pork, olives, nuts of any kind or seafood like shrimp, lobster and crab . . . you're probably going to die. If you're the type of woman who gives the silent treatment for any reason, you may find yourself . . . well, just say . . . Licences and permits are required from the home owner to take food into bedrooms. Some women, for some unknown reason, don't put toilet paper rolls on the dispenser. Why? Other women don't flush after a #1 . . . what's up with that? Not in my home.

I like food that is prepared with the use of a recipe. I don't just throw food together like a shit show. On another note, nothing but salt and butter on my popcorn, please. I eat mayonnaise, not salad dressing.

First thing I look for in a woman are the eyes. I am a back-end guy; neckline, shoulders, midriff, ankles and calves I find appealing. As I get older I'm becoming more attracted to chests. "B" to "G" are acceptable chest sizes. The sound of high heels as a woman crosses the floor arouses me.

I enjoy all foods. My vices are potato chips, bread and cheese. My social drinks are: a martini, a glass of wine or a shot (maybe 3) of spirit. I enjoy watching action, comedy and romance movies. I don't own a PVR. I am not fond of reality or talk shows. Shows like Housewives of anywhere, Oprah, Big Brother, Arrow, Castle, Flash, Grey's Anatomy, Gilmore Girls, soap operas, Master Chef, and America's Got Talent won't be on in my home. Even though I have watched them in the past to keep the peace, my view is that they are crap. I don't watch horror movies late at night because they affect my sleep. I will never watch or will there ever be conspiracy blogs on the internet in my home. They piss me off and make my blood boil. I don't want a woman who falls asleep or talks in a movie theatre. If you are a person who throws, drops or uses the remote control as a weapon, you will not be permitted to have it. Don't try to force me to watch your favourite shows, and should you ever change the channel I'm watching without my permission, consider yourself evicted. Mindless cartoons can play at other people's homes or theatres; parents put them on to shirk their responsibilities.

Even though I try to never say "hate," cigarettes and recreational drugs are at the top of my list of things I don't like. I've never had a cigarette or done a recreational drug in my life and I am proud of it. I don't and will NOT associate with people who do recreational drugs. Smoking of any kind or any so-called recreational drugs will NOT be permitted on my personal property. If you have an adult child over 25 who has failed at rehab, it may be necessary to put that child down.

I never will have anyone who is a member of or associated with the Hell's Angels in my home. I have never been fond of tattoos with the exception, for some reason, of a tattoo on a woman's lower back. I find those somewhat appealing.

I dislike crowded parking lots. As I stated earlier, I will do all the driving, as long as I'm capable, as I have been the passenger in six accidents in the past (ALL have been at the hands of female drivers). I'm a person who does not get mad easily, nor do I believe yelling is necessary in any relationship.

I don't appreciate it when people arrive at my home unannounced. Never park in front of my garage door without permission. Do NOT ever use my computer, and that's a funny one in itself, because 90% of what I do is on the iPad. I don't believe in owning any firearms. I do enjoy archery. I'm not a fisherman, but it is not a given that I won't be trying it in the future. I have a love and respect for animals. I will show common sense when decisions are made as an animal owner. "Diva" pets may be curbed along with their owners. Small, untrained barking dogs may disappear in the night. Yappy dogs raise my blood pressure. If you own a pet that dedicates on my floor . . . well, let's just say I like stir-frys of all kinds. No pets will be allowed in the kitchen or dining room, unless at my request.

Family and friends know I prefer Porsches, Ducati and Honda motorcycles and Ford trucks. Did you notice I said "prefer" and nothing about "afford"? I don't hang air fresheners or dreamcatchers from my rear-view mirrors, I feel they are distracting and trailer park-ish.

I like most genres of music. I primarily listen to blues, alternative and classic rock. I enjoy dancing, especially slow dancing, when I can gently press my hand in the small of her back while looking in her eyes. Kitchen dancing is amazing! The perfect woman will make me carrot cake, banana bread and cabbage rolls in the same week. I don't consider yelling and screaming music. I don't like, nor will I listen to, rap music. Music like Maroon 5 makes me go to the bathroom, when he sings in his upper register.

Punctuality is important. Don't make appointments you can't keep. That's why I will be in charge of my own wedding arrangements, should I get married again; once again, that is absolutely doubtful. I enjoy talking face-to-face. I use text messaging, cell phones and emails. I don't like Facebook and Twitter. I will NEVER use them unless my lawyer tells me to. I enjoy exercising in general: swimming, weight training, hockey, football and most physical sports.

Life can get bumpy at times and, like everything, relationships get shook up a bit. Life is a journey down a road that is always under construction. I want that perfect relationship. In public I say I have no regrets; I have many. I doubt all this crap means anything, as my sleep apnea and lack of a large package will prevent any long and meaningful relationship. The truth is that I've predicted my own passing for some time, with feelings that I've surpassed my importance and I doubt I will live past the age 65. Every night I go to sleep, I believe I'm not going to wake up. For the most part, I don't care if I die. Life is shit. I am not suicidal, though; I have too much respect for my friends and family to do anything like that.

Odan

Her coffee is half done and she's been gazing at the letter for more than fifteen minutes now. She looks up and sees Jon walk through the door, dressed in a blue windbreaker and jeans. He turns to his right and says, "Kelly, I'll be right with you," and then proceeds toward Trace. She turns the letter over, noticing he's getting closer. He asks her in a very calm, polite voice, "What are you up to, young lady? What brings you out here?"

She states, "I thought you would've heard by now, but I'm going to meet your father in a little bit."

"Why don't you join Kelly and me over at our table?" he asks in a hospitable voice.

She looks past Jon, over at Kelly, and says, "I'd love to but I've got some work to do first."

He gently taps his knuckles on her table with his right hand and says, "Well, you're more than welcome to join us when you're done," and walks away.

She stops him in his tracks and says, "Can I ask you a question?"

He stops and turns. "Okay. What's the question?"

"It's sort of close to the heart. Maybe you're not the person I should be asking," Trace says.

He replies, "Spit it out. I don't have all day and the worst I can do is say no." He comes back to the table and sits down. When she hesitates he says, "Listen, my dad is a lot of things, but he's been through hell and back and he doesn't deserve to be shit on."

He adds softly, "My dad is a funny guy, very witty with a big heart . . . and he just might be the most misunderstood person in the world. Don't mistake his kindness for weakness."

Trace asks reluctantly, "Is your family that funny or just that fucked up?"

"We're just dysfunctional, like every other family. I've got a dill hole of a half-brother who's no relation to my dad. I swear he's FAS . . . walks around all day pumped up on whatever street drug and juice he can find. I have an older brother I call 'Tender Flake' who has an eating disorder and outweighs my motorcycle. He spends half his time going LARP. I have two half-sisters who treat my dad like shit. No, no . . . let me take that back. All my siblings treat my dad like shit. I have a mother who has let herself go and is on her third marriage."

Jon continues, "I'm not sure if you're for real or just another futon. My dad told me a long time ago that I will treat women with respect. Me, personally, I make them sign a relationship agreement, in case it isn't reciprocated."

Trace replies with the question, "Am I supposed to understand what a futon is?" "After all that shit I told you, and the only thing you ask me is what a futon is? You'll catch on, and if you don't, it won't be important. Now, are you going to ask this badass question of yours, or are we going to continue to beat around the bush?" he asks.

She takes a second, has a drink of her coffee and leans forward before she says, "What drives him?"

"And here I thought you were gonna hit me with something earth-shattering and instead you ask a simple question that you should've figured out by now. That's easy . . . dreams! My dad is, was, and always will be a dreamer. And the biggest thing with that is . . . he's real."

Across the table, Trace searches Jon's face.

"I don't know what you've been told but it's plain and simple. Leave Ryker out of this, and oh . . . one more thing, he's my best friend. Yes, my dad is my best friend." Standing, he says, "I've got to go now. Kelly is waiting for me and we've got a full day ahead of us." He walks back to the table across the way with a rigid swagger.

Trace looks down at her seat and sees her cell phone vibrate. She thinks about it for a few seconds, looks up then reaches down and picks it up. With a note of reluctance in her voice, she answers, "Hello, Grayson?"

He sounds concerned. "I did some research on that fellow. There's a big . . . black mark at the government agency in regards to his parents, and I just received three mysterious calls ten minutes after I searched his name in the system. Something just doesn't add up," he says.

"I think his family might have a dark past. The second call I got, it was like it was the Cold War all over again. I hadn't heard the expressions 'go bag' and 'wet work' for a long time. Sorry to . . . So tell me, did you have your interview? How did it go? Is he good-looking?"

"The answer is yes, okay, and yes," she answers with a smile, then she tells him she has to go and they disconnect.

Across town, Odan is making a call from one of his cars, a silver C6 Corvette, while doing seventy-five miles per hour down the highway with the top off. The song by A Foot in Coldwater, "Make Me Do" has got him daydreaming. The phone rings.

"Hello, son, I hear you're having a bad day," he offers.

"No shit, Sherlock. It couldn't have gone any worse. Can I see you at the hangar?" he replies.

"What did you do now?" Odan questions with a parental sigh.

"Well, Dad, my mom is a bitch, Gary, too, and I just had a little fender-bender with one of your brand-new Ford half tons," he states in an overdramatic tone, like he always does.

"I told you to only use it for emergencies," Odan says. "It's brand-new and it only has a thousand miles on it."

Leif replies, "I just damaged the rear bumper."

"What the hell is wrong with you guys? That's three damaged rear bumpers in one week." Odan is steaming and it's heard in his voice as it cracks.

"I'm sorry, Dad. I'll be there just before nine at the hangar."

"That shit is coming off your cheque. You realize that this isn't the first time this has happened," Odan says.

"Love you, Dad. I'll see you there," Leif says indifferently.

Before he hangs up, Odan puts in, "Make sure you get all the pieces to Tom for that two-twenty-two before noon!"

Back in Detroit, Janice is on the phone again in her office.

"You can back your shit off or I'll bring my own wet work in," says the woman on the other end.

"Listen here, you pompous little bitch! I'll send it to you. Listen, I'll clean it up," says Janice.

"You don't stand a chance, you pencil pushin' twat, I know where he is," states the woman.

"And I know where you are," Janice replies.

The voice on the other end says after a delay, "It hasn't helped you so far, has it? By the way . . . when I'm done cleaning this shit up, I'm heading back there for a little housecleaning."

A warm breeze blows from the south as Trace pulls up to the front of the hangar in Mason just as it starts to drizzle again. To the right of the door, she notices two men are analyzing the damage to the back bumpers of three white Ford pickup trucks. Behind the trucks is a row of cars. An older man approaches her.

"I'm Tom," he states. "Come on and get out of the rain."

Inside the hangar it's dry and Trace takes the opportunity to look around. The hangar is meticulously clean. There are four planes on the left side and the right side is where the vehicles are parked. Between the vehicles and the planes is a path leading to the back of the hangar where there is a mezzanine made of metal and glass.

Tom points to his right and says, "These are Odan's babies. He doesn't collect art so, why not?"

He plays the tour guide and points out the automobiles, planes and their significance. "The big helicopter out front is an MI-26. It's from Russia. The largest in the world. He calls her Ruth. The plane beside it in white, blue and yellow is a P-68 Observer 2. The white-and-red twin 337 is a bird-dog, and the single engine is a 182 Stol. This black-and-silver truck on my right is called Stepchild, and it's the big guy's 'run around town' truck—it's a Ford F-50 with a 770 h.p. Coyote engine. The other vehicle he drives is kind of a beater. It's a silver 2008 Corvette. Everyone calls her Mona. That, over there," he says, pointing to a vehicle that is half covered up, "is his blue open-wheel sprint car that he hopes to race again soon. The wing of the sprint car has the name 'Wild Grandpa' written on it and the number sixty-nine. This here's his Porsche—he calls her Happy Foot. This is a grey SHO car he named Lorraine. The silver Saleen S7, red Rimac and the Maclaren 720s don't have names yet. The red Ducati ST3 motorcycle he calls Nicole."

"'To me they're just cars," pipes in Trace. "My husband, or should I say my ex-husband, likes Mercedes and BMWs."

They are about to climb the stairs to the mezzanine, when Odan appears. "I don't recall asking you what your thoughts were, nor do I care . . . Ms Scott."

Before Trace has the chance to respond, a man at the top of the stairs garners Odan's attention. "We need two Bambi buckets to the Cusp, ASAP," he says.

Odan replies leaning over the railing of the mezzanine to the hangar below, "Throw them in the back of my truck, Robby, and I'll run them out there in an hour and a half." He then casually walks over behind his desk, and as he does, she notices he's carrying a black book with white inserts on the front. He puts the book down, flips it over and starts writing something as he says to her, "So, what is it I can do for you?"

"I'm trying to get my head around whether there's a story to be had here or not," she says.

He replies, "There's nothing that hasn't been written before. Look, no offence to you, but I don't want my life on display for a bunch of jackasses to sit there and pick through it. I've already been down that road. I'm sure you're just trying to do your job so you can go on leading your little perfect white-picket-fence life, but I don't want any more drama or crap in mine."

"Can we not just make it a simple story about a small-town inventor?" she asks him politely.

"How are you going to get that done? I'm gonna tell you right now there is nothing black-and-white that I can tell you. My life up until this point has been full of colour . . . and not colour I'm particularly proud of. Not because of what I've done or not done. It's just that's the way things turned out. I made a lot of sacrifices in the name of family, and all I did was get shit on and knifed in the back in return."

"You seem like you're doing well for yourself now," she replies. "I see you with your family all the time, and business seems to be going well."

"Not all my family is around me—" he tosses back, "number one. And number two . . . it wasn't always like this." He puts his book down. He walks over to her, stopping less than four feet away and says, "I'm truly not interested in talking about the past. I'm making a concerted effort to move forward. I live life simply, try to do the best I can . . . I'm a bachelor, I do a load of laundry here and there, sometimes by hand."

He turns and walks back toward his desk. Just then Odan's son, Leif, walks in, looking mad. He says to his father, "That bitch! Sometimes I wish she would burn in hell! And the same goes for her dumbass Geritol husband!"

Odan replies, "What happened now?"

"Believe it or not, she went and told my soon-to-be ex-wife Monacunt where I'm banking with my girlfriend . . . even told her about my savings plans." Leif clenches his fists and stomps his feet. He continues, "Apparently they're out in Sundre riding horses. They're just doing what women do . . . talk, talk, talk, talk, talk, bullshit, bullshit, bullshit. Seriously, Dad, can we find a way to do them off?"

"Son, excuse me, this is Trace Scott. She's here looking to do an article on our dysfunctional family," Odan says, as he points in her direction with a candid smile.

Trace replies, "I saw you at the restaurant the other night and I've met your brother twice now, once just this morning."

"Oh, big fucking deal!" Leif spits. "What plastic tit horse did you ride up on? And what did that skinny little runt, Spike, have to say?"

"If you mean Jon, he was polite but short, and in a roundabout way was trying to give me directions," says Trace, as she gets out of the chair and starts walking toward the door.

Odan asks, "What directions was he trying to give you?"

With a smile, she says, "He was basically telling me where to go."

Odan holds his palm up to Leif and walks up to Trace and says, "Maybe we've been a little hard on you. It's been a bit stressful as of late and maybe . . . I can vent a bit. We can maybe do this. As long as you promise that I get to read whatever it is that you're writing before it hits print."

"Absolutely!" she says.

"Dad, you're not really gonna do this shit. She's just another twat trying to make money off your mistakes. Are you nuts?" Leif asks.

"Well, we can always bury her alongside your mother," Odan quips. They both grin, but Trace doesn't understand and it shows on her face. She looks up at Odan as he grabs her gently under the elbow and says, "I have to deliver these buckets. You might as well come for the ride." As she starts down the stairs in front of him, he says, "You understand that was just a joke, right?"

She looks at him over her left shoulder and says, "I sure hope so, or I'm going for a long ride."

He says with a grunt, "No, not long. She doesn't lie . . . I mean, live, far from here. Oops!" he exclaims suddenly. "I gotta run back and grab my journal. Just meet me in my little truck over there. It's open."

His phone rings as he enters his office. He glances at the incoming number. He picks it up and answers smoothly, "Hey there, Jordan. What can I do for you?"

"My wife is so pissed at me right now, so don't be surprised if you get a phone call," the man on the other end states anxiously.

"What did you do now? Am I gonna laugh?' Odan asks with a growing grin.

"Well, last weekend she became born-again. We had a disagreement and your name came up," Jordan states."

"Born again . . . when did she die? I would've been there for the party," Odan says, chuckling inside.

"Not funny, not funny at all. I'm the one who has to sleep with her," Jordan replies, giggling now."

"Face it, you're just too lazy to masturbate. Listen, I have to go. I gotta run some stuff out to the country and I have an unwanted guest I have to deal with," Odan says and then hangs up.

He skips down the stairs, missing every second tread, and walks over to the truck. Trace is sitting inside. He slides in and closes the door with a sense of confidence. He wraps the throttle and his cell rings again.

"I wondered how long it would take for you to call. I just got off the phone with your husband," he says in somewhat of a cavalier tone.

"I'm not happy right now and especially not with you," the woman on the other end says with a sharp tongue.

"And I'm sad right now . . . I heard you were born-again, and I didn't get a chance to deliver your eulogy," Odan replies quickly.

"I'm just going to ignore that right now—you're a bad influence. Jordan and I had a little spat last night and he said some things to me that weren't very kind. He called me a bad name," she says.

"Did he call you a bitch?" Odan asks, smiling over at Trace.

"No, he didn't," she replies in a confused tone.

"Did he call you a slut?" Odan asks, still looking over at Trace.

"No . . . not that either," she replies, the confusion in her voice growing.

Taking a moment to think about it, Odan stares straight ahead, twisting his hands on the steering wheel.

"Did he call you a cunt?"

"No! No, no, no!" she replies, her tone elevated.

"Well, that settles it . . . he didn't get it right," he says quickly with a big smile. "Now listen, I have to go to a brown-bear circumcision and a triple circle jerk and I'm running late. I'll have to catch up with you another time. Been nice chatting with you." He presses End on the call and they drive five minutes in silence.

Trace finally says, "Why is everybody so angry around here?"

"What do you mean?" Odan asks.

"Your son, Jon, gave me the death stare. Your other son, Leif, is choked with his mother, and one of your friends, Alan, threatened to punch somebody out in the parking lot the other day."

"Yeah, it's a bitch when their periods align," he replies, and continues, "but Leif didn't want to choke his mother, he wanted her to burn, if you recall."

"I'm not sure if that's meant to be funny," she replies.

"Oh, yes, from the steering wheel it is. When people ask me about my ex-wife, I don't tell them that I'm divorced, I just tell them I'd rather be a widower." They both smile.

Trace says, "This road is really rough and your truck . . . it's a little over the top, don't you think?"

"Reminds me of my past relationships," he says.

"Do you ever talk serious?" she asks.

"Only when I have to, or when I want to, and I'm not sure it's the time for either right now. Besides, it doesn't really matter."

They pull onto a service road and drive up to a matching blue-and-yellow fuel truck and helicopter.

"This is a Bell 222 UT, Ms Scott. We use it for a lot of the forestry work here. It's old and it's dependable," Odan states.

Two men approach the truck as Odan backs it up toward the helicopter. Odan gets out of his truck and helps the gentlemen unload the buckets. There is a thud when they hit the ground. The men shake hands and one of them does up the tailgate. Then Odan gets back in the truck. He pulls out the little black journal that is in the driver's-side map pocket. He opens it and makes a quick note inside. He closes it privately and replaces it in the map pocket. The display on the dash shows an incoming call from Jon Harrison. He pushes Answer and Jon says, "Where are you at?"

Odan replies, "We're on our way back from the Cusp."

"We?" asks Jon.

Just then, Trace gets a call and she has her phone on vibrate. She pushes Decline and gets a text message from her old boss, Grayson. A text comes through that reads:

Bad news. It has something to do with someone called The Tour Guide . . . She's out.

Trace replies:

How am I supposed to know what that's all about?

She waits for a reply, but it doesn't come.

Odan turns as his call is dropped and says to Trace, "Poor cell service here. I'll have you at your car in a couple minutes."

A few miles from the hangar, Trace's phone rings again. "Brother" is displayed on her cell. The text reads:

Where you be, little girl?

She replies:

Can't talk right now but I should be around in a little bit.

Brian texts back:

How about lunch today? There's a little place in town called Lokal. It's attached to a gas station near the lake. Can you make it there for high noon?

She replies:

Are you trying to sound like a damn cowboy? Lol. That shouldn't be a problem. I'll get directions.

Odan turns casually and in a very soft, almost submissive voice, he asks, "I have some errands to do and I have to stop by the school at three p.m. If you're not busy, you could give me a call after that."

He pulls up alongside of her car and she hesitates before answering. With a coy bite of the left side of her lower lip she says, "I think I'd like that, but is it okay if we do it a little later?"

"What's later?" Odan asks and says, "You do remember I have to go to bed early considering I'm an old guy, right?" He grins. She closes the door and he adds, "Well, as long as he's in bed . . ."

Although she doesn't understand, she says, "Sure." Then, still confused by that last statement, she jogs to her car. She gets in and starts driving back to her house. On the way, she pushes "Call Grayson" and the phone rings a couple of times before he picks it up.

"What was that text all about that you sent me"? she asks him.

He replies, out of breath, "I just copied and pasted what I got from some very special people in high places who do very special jobs."

"Why are you so out of breath?" she asks him.

"I'm running to the corner. Somebody hacked into our server last night and now we're trying to get everything up and running again. I hope this has nothing to do with your new boy toy," he replies.

"He's old," Trace replies, "and he's not my man toy."

She hears Greyson chuckle on the other end and says, "Thanks for the update. I have to run back to the house and grab some papers. I'm meeting Brian for lunch."

"Knock it out of the park," her former boss says, and she smiles as he hangs up.

Trace pulls into the restaurant parking lot. The dark skies have cleared up, leaving patchy pillows behind. The sun is almost directly above her, its fingers touching the tops of the adjacent fence. The restaurant is painted a bright green with black trim and has an old-school glass door. It's attached to a gas station and used to be a truck stop when the highway ran along the lake. Trace walks in, carrying a folder in her right hand while she fiddles with her keys, trying to stuff them in the back pocket of her frayed jean shorts. She spots her brother over in the corner. She walks over, smiling, even though he is looking down. The server leaves the table and takes both menus with her. She sits down and puts the folder beside her.

"Am I not going to get any food or am I on a diet? Do I look fat or something?" she jokes.

"No, no. The best thing here is either a steak or clubhouse, so I decided to order for you," he says.

"I guess you know me." She shrugs. "Would you mind telling me which one you ordered for me?" she asks.

"I ordered you a rare steak sandwich with salad and green tea," Brian replies stubbornly.

"Can I ask you why you're not in uniform?" Trace blurts out with her little sister attitude.

"I am in uniform. I just have some business to attend to. I rarely wear the uniform anymore," he continues and gives her a snide grin. "So, do I dare ask how your morning went with Odan?"

Coyly twisting a lock of hair around her finger, Trace replies, "Do me a favour and I'll tell you all about it?"

Smiling, lifting his coffee cup to his face, Brian says, "You do know, you're not supposed to flirt with your brother."

"I'm not. I'm sucking up. Can't you tell the difference, you ass?" Trace replies. The server brings her tea to the table and states, "Your food should be out shortly." The server is looking at Trace. She pays her no attention whatsoever, continuing to focus on Brian.

Brian replies for her, "Thank you very much," and their server walks away. Brian continues by saying, "Trace that was a little rude. Why didn't you acknowledge the server?"

"Sorry, I'm just a little long in the tooth from doing research on Odan. I haven't slept in a few days . . . at least, not well." Her eyes widen a little as she leans forward. "Dark horse" by Amanda Marshall plays in the background. Trace gently sways her head to an apparent favourite and continues, "I've been working on some very private character profiles of people in Odan's life. I need you to look at them and get back to me. In fact, I've even done one on you. I have no intention of publishing it, but I think this whole town has a shitload of colourful secrets. I have nowhere to turn, nobody to trust. I'm just trying to understand it." With her right hand, she passes some folded pages to him. He pulls a pair of glasses casually from his pocket and slowly opens the papers with both hands.

"What the hell, sis? You really haven't slept, have you? You can't keep doing this shit," he says, as he holds up the papers and shakes them. Brian looks back down at the paper. "Why do you need all this shit? Why?"

Staring back at him, Trace states, "Odan is colourful and so is his past . . . his friends, too. Please go over it for me?"

Profiles of Odan's dysfunctional family, friends, associates and crooks

Odan Harrison: Inventor. Passionate about music. Restaurant owner, owns Odan Harrison Projects, Rune Air, and Rune Ranches and Orchards. Witty and smart and a little crude. In his 40s. Born: Speedy Creek, Oregon. 6'1", 205 lbs. Thinning dirty blond hair in a Caesar cut. Blue eyes. Right-handed. Has a fair complexion and a strong jawline. Very athletic build and remains fit. Has a scar on his left ankle due to a motorcycle accident but it doesn't affect him. Played both football and hockey when he was in his teens. Charismatic, eclectic, funny alpha male. He is, well . . . he can be quixotic. Carries an aura around him. Truly a leader, not a follower. Some of his nicknames are Danimal, Danny Boy, Straw Dan, FLOTSCG (Fearless Leader of the Speedy Creek Gang) and Dyno. He is standoffish with women because of past relationships. His parents were Lutheran, but they never attended church. He was adopted at 1 or 2 years of age and was the last child adopted from an orphanage that closed down after his adoption. He was raised by a Danish family, Birthe and Hans Harrison. He was told his biological parents were Danish, as well. He is a meat-and-potatoes kind of man, but he enjoys lots of kinds of food, including rare steak and Asian food. He likes oatmeal for breakfast and his favourite type of egg is eggs Benedict. He has never had a drug, tattoo, or cigarette in his life and is not only proud of it, he is vehemently against all three. He drinks decaffeinated coffee with two cream because of his high blood pressure. Every day he has thoughts of dying. He has always felt alone in his relationships. The women in his life I have indicated he either talks too much or not enough. He is a sucker for potato chips and nuts. He listens to classic and alternative rock. He has been in relationships that didn't work out because of things he did, but has also been on the other side of the fence. He has been in half a dozen relationships where he thought the other person was "It." He has been badly cheated in business affairs, across a few different ventures and corporations. Has a two-month-old brindle Great Dane puppy named Barry and a three-month-old Nova Scotia duck tolling retriever puppy named Stanley. He has a warmblood horse named Bret. He drives a new black-and-silver Ford truck he calls Stepchild. He also owns a couple of motorcycles. Has extremely high blood pressure, sleep apnea and trigeminal neuralgia. Finally, he carries a little black diary with him everywhere he goes. I skimmed through two of his novels: *Playing with a Broken Moon* and *The Taste*. I wonder if he is this passionate or just has a great imagination.

Robert Barnes: Executive assistant to Odan Harrison. Born: Kalispell, Washington. 6'1". Right handed. Salt-and-pepper hair with glasses that date him and caring brown eyes. Has that vice-principal look. He has a very slight limp that has been with him all his life since childhood; he got it when he fell off a tractor. When he isn't doing manual labour, he wears a tie. A God-fearing man. As honest as the day is long. He has three adult daughters who have retained their belief in Christianity but have gone their separate ways, geographically. Very dedicated. He met Odan many years ago through business. He was the president of a corporation that owned intellectual property. He met Odan through a mutual friend and is now Odan's best friend. He, like Odan's other friends, drives a white Ford half ton.

Ryan Rochester: Sales manager at Odan Harrison Projects. 6'2" and 200 lbs. Right-handed. A strikingly handsome and tall, lean African-American man born in Ocho Rios, Jamaica. Raised in Ontario, Canada. Agnostic. He played briefly in the NFL. He then went and played in the CFL as a wide receiver until an ankle injury forced his retirement. He has a wife named Lizzy and three children: Mandy, Darla and Kyle. Close friend to Odan. Drives a red Nissan 370Z convertible like a little old lady.

Lizzy Rochester: Co-owner of The Lizard and Chicken (The Wet Spot) restaurant in Coldstream and The Karnivore Lounge in Mason with Odan. 5'9", beautiful with long brown hair and green eyes. Agnostic. Size nine shoes. Right-handed. Drives a new Mercedes SUV, black in colour.

Leif Harrison: Managing auditor of a government rehabilitation facility. Born: Innisfail, Washington. 5'9", 300 lbs. Red hair, blue eyes. Eldest son of Odan Harrison and his first wife Lynn Tobin. His daughter Morgan also has red hair. Ex-wife's name is Nicci or "Monacunt." He is patient, at times. He is also a closet pothead and has an eating disorder. Lost respect for his father a long time ago. Agnostic. Right-handed. Some years have passed since he lost his father's home, which he was residing in. He didn't make one payment in the year he was in the home. Some issues still remain in regards to his ex-wife removing all his father's belongings and claiming them as her own after the house was repossessed by the bank. Drives a dark blue VW Tiguan. Has a baby on the way with a coworker. Has difficulty answering straightforward questions and always has to throw in some dramatic statement in an attempt to appear intelligent.

Marie Harrison Secco: Owner of a hotshot business in Merit, Washington. Born in Innisfail, Washington. 5'6", 160 lbs. Strawberry-blond hair. Eldest daughter of Odan from first marriage with Lynn Tobin. Agnostic. Very strong-minded and stubborn. Became estranged from her father six years ago because of financial issues. She has a one-year-old daughter named Allys with her husband Titto, who is originally from Brazil. She hates Odan to the core. She wishes him dead. Her father wishes to rekindle his relationship with her. She drives a gold Expedition she bought with money from the family trust.

Neil Harrison: Wannabe tattoo artist and labourer. Born: Eckville, Washington. Has a recreational drug problem. 6', 200 lbs. Lazy. He was adopted by Odan when he was one year old. Right-handed. The son of Odan's second wife Leslie. Somewhat of an athletic body type. Not as strong as he believes he is. Bad temper. He is volatile and may have mental health issues. Has green eyes and a shaved head. His tattoo-covered body has multiple piercings. Atheist. Has a Grade Eight education but is a real know-it-all. Has read more in the last two years than he read in the previous twenty. He has bully tendencies. He does not get along at all with his brother Jon Eric. Jon calls him "Little Dick." He is loud and abrasive. Has two male children, Logan and

Kenny, from two different mothers but born on the same day. He hates Odan. He has tried many jobs but because of his lack of education he is restricted to the construction industry. He drives a blue and green 1971 Ford half ton, registered in his wife's name, that is in terrible shape and burns oil, but he doesn't have a driver's licence.

Jon Eric Harrison: Design consultant for Odan Harrison Projects. Born: Eckville, Washington. 6'2", 180 lbs. Very lean. Has long, slender arms and thin, long legs. Suffers from a right shoulder injury from a bicycle accident. Atheist. Right-handed. Receding dirty blond hair. Brown, honest eyes set farther apart than his siblings'. Gentle heart. He is the biggest eater in the family and could easily eat every half an hour all day long. He has a quick temper and dislikes his half-brother Neil. He was working at trying to rekindle his relationship with his father, but he gave up. His hobbies include tech, blacksmithing and spelunking. Would like to be like his father. Always seeking the approval of others. Holds resentment about the way his siblings have treated his father. Calls his eldest brother "Tenderflake," and wishes he would get in shape. He has tattoos he wishes he never got. He is the most evolved of Odan's children. Has a son named Julian who he calls "Skidmark." He takes pride in a 2010 Ford van he converted into an RV. Thinks Neil is a thief and has become paranoid because of him. Type One diabetic. Drinks Komodo Dragon coffee and puts an ice cube in it. Uses the expression "dill hole" a lot.

Stephanie Harrison: Was home sales representative for Odan Harrison Projects until fired by Robert Barnes.

Born: Condor, Washington. 5'7", 190 lbs. Brunette, long wavy hair. Janitor. Has beautiful round green eyes. Could be a model if she lost weight. Right-handed. Chain-smokes and gambles in excess. Couldn't care less whether her father lives or dies. Has two children with her fiancé, Grady Trent: a boy named Tristan and a daughter, Elena. Atheist. Listens to a lot of country music and eats very plain food. Isn't much into spices. Drives the silver Escape her father, Odan, gave her from the family trust.

Dawn Harrison: Runs a group home for children with learning disabilities. Born: Rocky Mountain House, Washington. 5'5", 140 lbs. Blond with similar character traits and appearance to her half-sister Marie. Has a son, Dakota, born with Down syndrome who is ten. Atheist. Never has anything positive to say about her father. Drives a red Ford Escape that her father, Odan, gave her from the family trust.

Danton Harrison: AKA Man-cub, Goo, Golden Child. Labourer on a construction crew in the pipeline industry. Born and still lives in Rocky Mountain House, Washington, with his grandmother. 5'9", 155 lbs. Dark hair and brown eyes. Odan's youngest son. His mother is Esme Kingsinghe, originally from Sri Lanka. His grandfather was a doctor in Rocky Mountain House, but has since passed away. Danton is spoiled and pampered by grandmother Kandy Kingsinghe. Atheist. Has tattoo of his first real girlfriend on his right side. Holds very little respect for Odan because of unfulfilled dreams due to unsuccessful business ventures. Has a habit of mumbling and not speaking clearly or loud enough at times. Drives a white Ford truck he received from the family trust. Has a small collection of tuner cars that he's proud of because he bought them with his own money.

Cereana Greenwood: AKA Lucy Fir or Happy Foot. Parts manager at a recreation equipment company in Mason. Born: Salt Lake City, Utah. 5'2", 159 lbs. Struggles with her weight. Size seven shoes, medium-length blond hair, soft teal eyes, double-D breasts. Has a daughter named Patience in college in Boise, Idaho, studying adolescent psychology. Eyebrows are one shade darker than her hair. Has a tattoo of a rose on her left shoulder. Atheist. Wears contact lenses. Always wears Lululemon. Quite often wears an old volleyball jersey from her high school in Salt Lake City, # 6. Little round nose. Very curvy physique. Her voice is a little nasally and higher-pitched than most. She had feelings for Odan once; Odan thinks she's a sweetheart. Atheist. Craves carbs and especially loves pizza, Thai, steak and crab. Allergic to some nuts but not peanuts. Listens to Maroon 5, One Republic, Fleetwood Mac and Foreigner. Has an orange cat named Karma. Drives a new pewter Ford Fusion.

Alan Harvey: Owns a fabrication shop in lake country. 6', 230 lbs., balding and almost always wears a ball cap in public. Wears off-the-shelf glasses. Catholic. Has a little belly that's been growing over the years thanks to his wife's cooking. Put the pepper on the table and watch him sneeze. Always jokes about being in better shape and lighter than Odan but he isn't. His moustache is growing grey and has stains from years of smoking. Just about always wears a shirt that has a pocket for his cigarettes. He's a salt-of-the-earth type of man—honest and would give you the shirt off his back. Been known to get silly after two much rum. Treats Odan poorly every time he gets drunk. Strangers are always welcome at his home for dinner. He enjoys hunting and fishing with his two boys, Jesse and Ian. Ian isn't around much, due to work. As a teenager, Alan was in the army. He was a good marksman. His daughter Eva is a pharmacist in the nearby town of Lumby. Alan had been a Dodge man for many years but now drives a Ford half ton. He is one of Odan's closest friends although the relationship is strained every time Al gets drunk. Al never apologizes and that bothers Odan.

Gwen Harvey: Co-Owns Dawn Eva's Greenhouse and Orchard in lake country and Springfield Market in Mason, with her daughter. Born: Saskatoon, Saskatchewan. 5'2". Shoulder-length brunette hair. Blue eyes. Has a big contagious smile and a warm personality. Catholic. Epitomizes the farm girl. Wears blue jeans most of the time and shorts when it is extremely hot. Met her husband in a Firestone tire shop 30 years ago. She is a great cook and baker. Has a very curvy physique. Known as the backbone of her family. She is the only one in her family who doesn't smoke cigarettes. In the spring, summer and fall you can find her in the garden or the greenhouse. Drives a two-tone orange Land Rover Evoke that she won in an agricultural competition.

Walter Wayne: Finance specialist. Born: Outlook, Saskatchewan. 6'1", 195 lbs. Balding, white hair. Blue eyes behind wire-rimmed glasses and a full, manicured moustache that covers his top lip. Has very fair skin. Christian. Spends a lot of his time on various charitable boards. When conversing, he frequently grooms his moustache with the fingers on his left hand. Has a big smile and a big laugh. Enjoys golfing and he and his wife travel extensively. A very generous man but friends joke with him about his frugal nature. He was a good friend with Odan until he undermined him. Drives a black Ford 350.

Khup: Runs Bamboo Specialty Corporation, Ltd. for Odan. From Mandalay, Burma. Talks too much.

Tyson (Ton): Playboy businessman from Vietnam, struggling to get his business off the ground.

Gary Wallace: Owns Leathead Auto Body in Coldstream. Born: Niverville, Manitoba. Salt-and-pepper hair, 5'9" and 180 lbs. Steel-blue eyes. Has separate glasses for business and for pleasure. Normally dresses in dark-coloured jeans with a wind breaker, bright yellow shoes and a blue shirt. Has a scar on his right knee from having surgery. Very much a car guy and always will be. Atheist. Very witty. Always positive. Has two career-driven adult daughters. One of his daughters works with him at his shop and the other is a nurse. He is a close friend to Walter and always has the ability to get under his skin. They enjoy travelling to Mexico every chance they get. He was a friend of Odan's. Drives a grey Audi Q5 and deep metallic slate-grey Audi R8.

Helen Scott: Mom, housekeeper and writer. Born: Coldstream, Washington. 5'6", 140 lbs. Athletic, model-type body. Eats right and takes care of herself. Agnostic. Sharp facial features and large cat-shaped green eyes. Played all the sports in school; was captain of her university volleyball team. She likes to wear sundresses in earth tones or light colours. Has two children: Brian and Trace. Married to Arthur Scott. Drives a Subaru Forrester.

Arthur Scott: Dad. Retired road builder. 6' and 200 lbs. Dirty blond hair going grey. Agnostic. Strong build from playing football through college. Full eyebrows with dark close-set blue eyes. Has a tattoo of a bear on his right arm that he got after an encounter that killed his best friend when they were younger, clearing the land. Wears shirts that show his arms and chest, in mostly grey or green. He drives a brown mid-'90s Chevy three-quarter-ton truck.

Kelly Ranger: Building contractor for Odan Harrison Projects. 5'9", 180 lbs. Stocky carpenter with a big heart. Dirty blond hair, hazel eyes and a rugged jawline. Always has a two-day-old growth of facial hair. Atheist. Good-looking man with back problems due to many years in the construction industry. Has a big, slightly crooked smile and his whole body moves when he laughs. Met Odan years ago through associates in regard to a German-castle type home he built for a client. Kelly and Odan are close friends, and seem to share the same views on construction and design. Kelly likes archery. He drives a company white Ford half ton. He uses the expression "working and killing time" a lot. On the phone he calls Odan a "bed-wetter" with a snicker.

Dean Watson: Utility line project manager. Fifty-five years old. 6'1", 230 lbs. Been at the same utility line corporation for 40 years. Very short dirty-blond greying hair and blue eyes. Agnostic. He was a good friend of Odan for fifteen years.

David Lorrie: Retired professor of 18th-century German history. Born in Frankfurt, Germany, then moved to Mason. 5'5", bald, 135 lbs. Blue eyes. Pencil-thin fair eyebrows. Professional thick-rimmed glasses with blue trim. Lean physical stature. Christian. Has prominent but not large ears. In a wheelchair due to an automobile accident 10 years ago. Speaks very clearly and slowly with an old German accent he acquired from teaching 18th-century German history. Quirky. Spends a lot of his time in rehab working on regaining his balance and motor skills. Drinks his coffee with a little half-and-half. Mason is where he met his friend Odan. He drives a copper Honda Element.

Brian Scott: Brother. Dick. Chief of police of Coldstream. Born: Coldstream, Washington. 6'2", 230 lbs. Blond thinning hair and judgmental blue eyes. Eyebrows that are a bit darker than his hair. Agnostic. Has a habit of staring during conversation. His police unit is a dark grey Tahoe. His personal car is a Shelby Mustang.

Raymond: Owner of many properties and oil and gas companies. 6'1", 195 lbs. Half Irish, half Métis. Full head of grey hair. Blue-green eyes behind a pair of all-business wire-rimmed glasses. Talks in a growl, never talks monotone. Sharp casual dresser. Walks totally upright and fast, with a purpose. Has a firm hand shake. Some say he's only friends and business partners with Odan because of Odan's ideas. Owns Ramco. Drives a white Ford Limited half ton.

Lynn Tobin: Hospital kitchen worker. Born: Innisfail, Oregon. 5'5", 170 lbs. Curly shoulder-length blond hair, blue eyes. Odan's first wife. Is a good mother but not a good person. After divorcing Odan she married Gary Tobin. She is a very dishonest person. She hates Odan and holds only spite for him. Drives a blue Jeep Wrangler.

Tommy Couture: Bush pilot and retired musician who subcontracts out to AAT for firefighting. Has a wife and two children and enjoys flying. Born in Flin Flon, Manitoba. He thinks he is a singer.

Cory Mac: From Saint John's, Newfoundland. Runs a toy store, and his wife runs a toy store that competes against him in a small town nearby. A huge Montréal Canadiens hockey fan. Coaches a hockey team that Odan sponsors. They played hockey together once upon a time.

Jeff Hammond: Helicopter pilot. Subcontracts out to AAT for firefighting. Married twice. Has two daughters from his first marriage and twin sons from his second marriage. He thinks he's funny. Born in Dallas, Texas.

Peter Derickson: Financial planner. 6'2", 220 lbs. Dark short hair. A very crooked man with a deceptively trusting look. Wife is a drug addict. He has two children, both of whom have left home and no longer speak to him. Phony dresser. Has undermined many people's businesses. He ran Odan's first aircraft company into the ground by pretending he would do investor relations and then backstabbing him. Drives a black Jeep SRT. Bought a fully restored red '57 Chevy. Basically, a piece of shit excuse for a human being.

Esme Kingsinghe: Waitress at a Pizza Hut restaurant. Born: Rocky Mountain House, Washington. 5',150 lbs. May have been pretty when she was 18. Long black hair starting to go grey and large dark eyes. Mole in the left crease of her nose. Has been spoiled all her life. Has always gotten by on her looks but age is rapidly closing in on her. Chain-smoker and drinker. Red wine and rye whisky with coke are her drinks of choice. Cannot be alone and makes poor personal choices. Has lied to her son about many circumstances in regards to Odan. She has another son named Nathaniel from another relationship. Has a green General Motors pickup truck in her backyard, missing one headlight and a tailgate. It sits idle because she can't drive it due to an impaired driving charge.

Watt Robby: Plant cleaning equipment company owner. 5'8",165 lbs. Beady eyes behind wire-rimmed glasses. A follower who has been led astray by others who use him to do their dirty work. Car collector and associate of Peter Derickson. Pled guilty and was convicted of bribing officials. Helped Peter Derickson screw Odan. Drives a deep-blue Cadillac four-door sedan.

Lisa Jackson: Investment broker. 5',130 lbs. African-American. Married with one daughter, Jada. Originally from Reynolds, South Carolina. Now lives in Lithia Springs, Georgia.

Catarina Wanderbelt: Investment broker. 5'5",145 lbs. Blond hair, blue eyes. Half Dutch, half German. She has a son, Dennis, from her first marriage. Her hobbies are painting and dressmaking. Mike Schlossor was her common-law husband. Resides in Madrid, Spain. Has a partner named Christian.

Gary Adelle: Publisher of newspaper and magazine, *Naramata*. 70 years old. 6', bald, designer glasses. Big mouth and smile. Has dark eyebrows and a few lines on his face. Was in business at one time with Peter Derickson and things did not end well. Good energy, but stabbed Odan in the back in business. Has a criminal record as a minor for arson and criminal negligence.

Edwin Henry: Was a homebuilder for Odan Harrison Projects. 6'1", 265 lbs. Born in the same hospital as Odan in Speedy Creek, Oregon. Receding salt-and-pepper hair with more salt than pepper. Honest hazel eyes, with full, grey eyebrows. Tough and strong build with very large hands. Very firm handshake. Drives a white Ford half ton. Has six grandchildren from four children. Edwin has a wife named Deb, whom everyone calls Daisy. Deb was a dental hygienist until four years ago when she fell off of Ed's snowmobile. She wasn't badly hurt, but now she spends most of her time as a housewife and paints nude male oil paintings.

Fredrick Olason: Owns a road-building company. 6' and 280 lbs. A jolly, well-kept businessman who has spent his life in the construction industry building highways. Has a full head of grey hair, blue eyes and fashionable glasses. Has that down-to-earth way of talking that comes from being half-Scandinavian and half-Ukrainian. Business associate and partner of Odan's.

Donna Annley: Police constable in Mission. 40 years old, 5'3" with dark hair. Has been a constable in the fraud department for 15 years. Crooked. Married and has a business degree she acquired before entering the police force. Having an affair with Linda Anderson's employer, Derrick. Has a hate-on for Odan.

Book: Aviation broker. Born: Lynn Lake, Manitoba. 5'9" with wire-rimmed glasses and blue eyes. Has a full head of salt-and-pepper hair. Was at the top of his game 20 years ago. Has a wealth of knowledge about aircraft. Starting to make mistakes because of pressure from creditors. Kind heart, tries to fit in everywhere. His right eye tears up when he is excited or under stress.

Gregg Nazzari: Odan's corporate lawyer. 5'5",140 lbs. Sharp Italian attorney who looks after Odan's corporate affairs. Has short, balding blond hair, blue eyes and a quick smile. Wife is a tall blonde and they have two children. Drives a grey Audi S7 and a bright-red Audi R8. Favourite saying is "Pigs get fed and hogs get slaughtered." Has, like a lot of people, lost faith in Odan. Odan gets pissed off when Greg doesn't return his calls.

Tarissa Grey: 5'1",124 lbs. Concerned about her fluctuating weight. Short blond hair, blue eyes. Owns an interior decorating store in Summerland. Delivers for Skip the Dishes part-time. Divorced the first time due to infidelity. Divorced the second time because of the strained relations between her children and her husband. Has 5 children, a couple of whom have issues; the boys are now trying to better themselves. Also has 4 grandchildren. Says the wrong things at the wrong time. Spends a lot of time with a friend named Rita. Leans on the Bible, but won't put her foot down with her children. Has three adult children over 25 living at home. Gossips too much. Drives a light-green Escape. Her emotions and feelings for Odan are on again, off again, like the weather. Her family doesn't like Odan because of false accusations made about him.

Aaron Klassen: Musician. Owns a lounge in Canmore, Alberta. Has longer hair. Married with 4 children. He cowrote music with Odan years ago that was never published.

Ronnie Van: Redheaded pilot that Odan fired due to trust issues. Odan believes he stole jewellery from him.

Jason Camps: Viticulturist, played in a band when he was much younger and wrote music and is very passionate about wine. Lost a testy to a quail bite. Wears a hat and is very self-conscious about going bald. Has a wife, daughter and a Great Dane dog named Stella.

Channi C.: Manager of The Lizard and Chicken. Tall brunette, 5'7", drives a cherry-red Acura NSX and a Ducati Monster. Has five sisters, including a married twin sister who has four children and lives on a farm in North Carolina with her husband. Her vice is five-cent candy. Doesn't eat omelettes in the morning because they bother her stomach. Doesn't like anyone to put their feet on her. Finished hair-dressing course (doesn't use it). Rocks out to Nickelback to get in the groove when on a mission. Plays hockey and shoots right. Also has a sister who is an MMA fighter (Holly-fire). Had trouble in school in English but has persevered and always has a positive attitude.

Richard Stoes: 6'1", 180 lbs. Real-estate agent specializing in foreclosures. Has a wife and two teenage children. Short, thinning, dirty blond hair. Drives a red Toyota Camry hybrid. Left-handed and never wears a belt on his pants. Loves to golf and does it as much as he possibly can. Has a scar on his hand from a home renovation accident.

Bob Sherrit: 5'9", 180 lbs. Bright green eyes. Retired motorcycle state trooper. Avid activist for motorcycle safety. Has a heart of gold. He's a supporter of cancer fundraising events, including rides for awareness. Drives a teal Subaru Forester and gold Honda motorcycle.

Louise: 5'4" with long, brown, slightly greying hair. A close friend of Odan's and takes care of some of his books for him. Left-handed. Has 6 daughters and recently divorced. Soft, kind eyes and an approachable demeanour. Odan spends a lot of his downtime with her. She previously worked with Odan. Recently parted with her boyfriend from Jamaica. Clumsy. She's a nanny now.

Perry: Property management business owner. Ripped Odan off.

Rebecca: Friend of Stephanie. Horse-riding instructor. Large warm brown eyes behind bold-framed glasses. 5'4", full-figured, struggles with weight issues, but very attractive. Has a bun in the oven and two children: a three-year-old boy Odan calls "T-Rex" and a one-year-old daughter named Tag. Rebecca is a sex addict. She is bisexual and an old hippie soul.

Todd Nosrednas: Accountant. Two children, married twice. Bald, 6'1", enjoys cycling but has health issues. Odan stopped using him; he could have stood up for Odan but chose not to do the right thing. Drives a red Jaguar ragtop.

Sunny Arbrednow: One of Odan's accountants. Very pleasant and a single mother of three. Has secrets. Drives a white Ducati motorcycle and a Nissan sports car.

Emily Daniels: AKA Bush Bunny, Granny. Widow. Sensitive green eyes. Natural brunette but dyes her hair to avoid the grey. High, distinctive eyebrows. Drives a white Jeep Summit SUV. Glazed tan, 5'5", 120 lbs. Wears complimentary tight-fitting clothes, mostly black-and-white stripes. Four grandchildren (all boys). Allergic to certain nuts and dairy, and sensitive to gluten. She has a small purebred Havanese. Jaded and unlikely to ever marry again. Was wrongfully accused of manslaughter. She despises her ex-daughter-in-law (daughter of Tarissa Grey). She has been divorced twice and widowed once. Lost her only son to cancer. Her son-in-law is a small-time thug.

Stacey Ann: Odan's part-time lawyer. Barbie doll.

Doug Lambert: Odan's patent and trademark attorney. Practices and resides in Victoria. 6' with salt-and-pepper hair. Very well spoken. Used to run marathons. Drives a black Mercedes SUV and a Mini. Odan trusts him.

Chris Segrof: A lawyer for Odan's commercial enterprises and Raymond's go-to lawyer. Smokes cigars. A little cranky.

Dana Nosirac: Playboy lawyer; does Odan's family law. Does most of it with a bottle of wine in his hand.

Darrin O'Liar: A lawyer who worked for Odan at one point in time and has now branched out.

Nicci Blaim: Redhead. Glasses. 160 lbs. The mother of one of Odan's grandchildren and the ex-wife of Leif. Short-fused and spends most of her time LARPing. Doesn't take care of herself. Odan still treats her like his daughter and thinks her shit doesn't stink.

Dr. M.C.: Odan's physician. From Pretoria, South Africa. Early thirties. Tall and thin with dark hair. Comes from an affluent family. Appears to be very close to Odan.

Judge Wellington: Old. Someone should hang that cranky prick.

Jeff Marshall: Small-town drug dealer. Has a son from a previous relationship. Sells steroids to police and prison guards. Spends his time bad-mouthing Odan.

Across town, a call comes in on Odan's cell from "Bubba."

"Can I have him for the next three days?" the female voice on the other end asks into the receiver, as he manoeuvres his truck through the downtown traffic.

"Ryker has kindergarten Monday and Wednesday . . . He hasn't been sleeping well lately, so I want him in bed by 8:15," he responds.

Odan attempts to hit all the green lights and stay in the right-hand lane. He notices a police car behind him, following his every move. On the Bluetooth he is still talking to the individual on the other line but now he has changed his tone to one that's much stricter.

"I won't tolerate any BS or variances on the conditions that I've already established . . . period."

"Does that mean I get him for the weekend?" the woman on the other end asks.

Odan replies, "I'll draft an agreement prior to him spending overnights. It will be black-and-white and I fully intend to enforce it in its entirety."

"You're an ass and you know it," the woman says.

"Yes I am, but that . . . that little boy's heart is more important to me. I'll leave Kuusamo at seven o'clock tonight and pick him up at seven forty-five a.m. tomorrow," Odan states. He drives for a block in silence.

The voice on the other end reluctantly says, "Sure, that'll work." Then she adds, "But text me the details so I have it in writing."

She hangs up without waiting for an answer. Odan sits in his truck at a the light, watching two trucks pull their boats through the intersection and gazes over his right shoulder into the box of his truck, noting that one arrow is still there. He pushes "Trace" on his cell. His nervous anticipation has him rubbing the seam of his jeans with his right hand. It's difficult for him not to feel the tightness on the front of his jeans as the call is completed.

"Trace here," she answers in a happy, giddy voice.

"Hey, Odan here," he says.

"I'm just wrapping up lunch with my brother," she states.

"He didn't buy you a clubhouse, did he?" Odan asks.

"Why do you ask that?" she asks.

He replies, "He's a tight ass . . . Can I interest you in a glass of wine this evening?"

Trace stumbles through her response, "If I was asked and I had nothing to do, it could maybe be a possibility."

"Well, it's official. I'm asking you . . . if that works for you?" he inquires.

Trace replies in a nervous voice, "Just one glass . . . maybe two."

"That's gonna be your call," Odan says.

"At your restaurant?" she asks, and cheekily adds, "You're the only one that I can skip out on the bill on."

Trace looks up at her brother with a condescending glare. Brian is observing some pretty friendly bantering back-and-forth and, still on the phone, holds up his finger to Trace and wiggles it back-and-forth disapprovingly.

"Yeah, what the hell! I'd love to. I'll see you at your restaurant at 7:15," she says to Odan, smiling at her brother.

"Why don't you swing by my place at six and we can go together?" Odan suggests.

"I don't know where you live," Trace says.

"117 Kuusamo Crest. It's down the Rainy Creek Road," he explains in his quiet, confident tone.

"Is that easy to find?" Trace asks.

"Not too easy . . . and that's the way I like it," he replies. "And I hope you don't mind, but I have to drop off my little one at his bubba's before we go."

"What do you mean, 'little one'?" Trace asks, her curiosity piqued.

"My five-year-old, blue-eyed blond boy, Ryker. I gotta go now. I got another call coming in," Odan says.

"You can explain it to me when I get there . . . see you then," she says as a sigh escapes her.

"Well . . . I guess that's my cue. I'm outta here." Abruptly, she gets up and walks away from the table, leaving her brother speechless. Her mind is swirling, trying to figure out what she should wear, as she climbs into her car. Wrinkling her nose, she turns on the engine and cranks the music. The drive goes by in a blur, and she parks her car and runs into the house, where she scampers like a fourteen-year-old to her room. She looks in the closet and decides on a summer dress. A white one with tangerine trim. A dress that has been sitting in the closet since she last left. She doesn't notice that the sundress is a little translucent. The light in the bedroom isn't as revealing as the sun. Her ruby-coloured bra and thong show through the thin material. She has a shawl that she brought with her from New York that has bronze tassels, and she throws that overtop. Then she scampers back down the stairs. Her gait is quickened by her ragged breath and rapidly beating heart.

Trace drives her car down the five miles of gravel at pavement speed to get to a subdivision nestled on the south-west corner of the lake. The road turns left here and the pier is straight ahead. She follows it to the second house on the right. It is a sprawling stone bungalow, with a turret on the right. There are two parking levels, and she parks on the upper one. She walks down and there's a wrought-iron gate. She pushes it open and it creaks. She leaves it open and follows a stone path to the front door. She gathers the hem of her summer dress in her left hand and pushes on the door chime. She looks to the right and spots her reflection in the window, and for the first time she notices that her outfit is more revealing than she thought. He opens the door and welcomes her in.

Stepping inside, she struggles to keep herself from staring at Odan, who is dressed in a blue dress shirt that matches his caring eyes. His steel-grey blazer with pinstripes outlines his athletic build. His faded tight blue jeans and light-brown alligator shoes complete his attire.

"Welcome, welcome!" he says. "Come in and make yourself at home." Trace hears the voice of a young male child playing in the room adjacent to the dining room. She puts her keys on the chair beside the door and walks cautiously ahead. Glancing around, she notes that the house is meticulous. There are details that should not be found in a bachelor's home unless there is professional help in maintaining it. A bookshelf to the right of the door holds a collection of eclectic books from different periods and on different subjects. A children's book, *Benjamin and Floosy*, sits beside two of Odan's books, *Playing with a Broken Moon* and *Forget Me Knot*, on the lower shelf. The balance of the house is open concept, decorated in a blend of pastels and earth tones. Black-and-white photographs of children adorn the walls. The west side of the great room is sparsely but tastefully decorated with leather furniture framing the living room area.

As Odan get his little boy ready to go, she asks, "Am I okay to continue looking around?"

Odan replies, "Yes, of course. I'll be a few minutes yet, and then we can be off. No one ever won a horse race by saying 'whoa.'"

She walks to her left through the great room to the open doorway of the master bedroom. She peeks in, then decides to step inside. The master bedroom is very large with an en suite at the other end. The king-size bed and furnishings are done in a grey distressed wood accessorized with black hardware. Trace walks over to the closet and gently slides the barn door open to reveal all of Odan's clothes colour-coordinated, starting with black on the far left. His shoes are organized in the same way. She closes the closet door and heads out across the living room to the base of the spiral staircase heading above. She passes through a small area where there are guitars hung on the wall and she notices one says "Rickenbacker" and one says "Gretch." She proceeds upstairs to the lookout, holding on to the railing with care. She gets to the top rung and notices three books centred on a stunning eight-foot etched-glass desk with deep-red chairs flanking it on either side.

Odan calls out from the floor below, "I have two pups—a retriever and a Dane— but they're out at the farm right now or I would introduce you to them." She recognizes the book on the far right. It is the one Odan has been carrying around. Her curiosity gets the best of her and she glances over her shoulder then gently leans closer to get a look at the book. On the cover are the initials, "WYD." She turns it over and it says "5918," so she turns it back to its original side. She takes a step away and stops. She turns around and decides to open the book. In the middle of the first page she sees the words, "Lynn—burn in hell," and on the page across from it, it says, "Judge— hung.'" Rob—crushed" is written on another page . . . and there are other allusions to what sound like deaths. She thumbs through the journal quickly, then she closes the book and puts it back exactly how she found it.

Odan shouts up the stairs, "Ready to go in five!" and, realizing she has more time, she goes back and takes one more look inside the book. She notices that one part of the book is filled with aircraft terminology, while the other part of the journal is riddled with those names. She puts the journal back in place and looks out over the lake. The office is in a round turret that rises nine feet higher than the house. There are half a dozen boats two hundred feet out from the shoreline, with families pulling tubes and skiers. She can see the opposite shoreline approximately two miles across. The sun reflects off cabin windows onto the lake.

Odan's voice echoes through the house, "It's time to rock 'n' roll." Trace looks around the turret before she starts down the spiral stairs, putting her left hand on the rail. At the bottom of the narrow staircase she notices initials carved into the wood at the base of the rail. A quick look inside the kitchen and she sees it is tastefully appointed with stainless steel appliances. They have those same red knobs as her parents' home.

"Are you coming?" Odan says. "We have two stops to make before we hit the restaurant."

"Sorry," Trace says, coming around the corner.

Odan replies, "I wasn't talking to you . . . my bad. I'm just trying to get the little guy's attention."

Ryker comes running out from the other room. "Dyno . . . Dyno . . . Dyno!" the little blond-haired blue-eyed boy shouts. He runs right past Odan out the door and heaves open the truck door, scrambling into the middle seat and buckling himself up. "Let's go, Dyno!" the tiny voice shouts from the truck.

"How about that? Now we're the ones holding him up." Odan chuckles and Trace smiles up at him as she puts on her shoes.

Through the garage door, she spots a pair of compound bows hanging on the garage wall. She asks, "Are you an archery guy?"

"Used to be," he replies, "but I just can't find the time anymore . . . between work and the little guy. I haven't used them for years." They walk briskly toward the truck and a breeze comes up from behind them and blows the scent of lilac toward them. The last vestiges of sun dance on the silver stripes on the truck's hood.

"So what's the plan?" Trace asks as she closes the door behind her.

Odan replies, "We are going to—briefly—stop by a construction site, then we're going to drop Ryker off at his grandma's. From there, we're going to head up to the restaurant for a glass of wine and a little seafood, if that works for you?"

"I guess . . . I don't have a choice, do I? I'm buckled in already," Trace replies as she looks at him with a girlish smile. Ryker reaches and turns on the stereo. A Rob Thomas song comes on.

The little boy looks up at Trace and says, "He plays this music all the time."

"Not *all* the time," Odan replies, grinning.

They drive for about four miles into a new subdivision as the sun is going down. They pull up on a dirt pad behind two white F150 Ford trucks. A new rock fascia modern house is under construction beside an empty lot. On the other side of the lot is another big partially constructed contemporary house; in all there about a dozen houses at different stages of completion. There is a black SUV parked on the empty lot beside the houses they are now in front of. Two men walk out of the house. Odan turns his truck off and steps out. "Dyno," the little boy asks, tilting his head back and looking up with his kind eyes, "can I stay in the truck?"

"Yes, you can. We're not going to be out of sight," Odan says.

Odan tells Trace to get out and the two of them walk toward the men. "This is Trace," Odan says by way of introduction.

"We know who she is," says the shorter man. He reaches out to shake her hand. "Hello, my name is Kelly." He looks at Odan and says, "She's even hotter up close."

A warm blush comes over Trace's face and Odan clears his throat and makes an attempt at changing the subject. "Kelly, did we pour the concrete today?" he asks, as they walk toward the garage.

The other man, who Trace recognizes as Odan's son Leif from their volatile meeting at the airplane hangar, is now partially alone with Trace and says to her in a quiet voice, "I talked to Spike today."

She asks in a confused tone, "Why do you call Jon, 'Spike'?" She shuffles a bit to the side and kicks a small board off a stone.

Leif says, "That's what we used to call the skinny bastard brother of mine back when he had hair."

"Does this mean you've changed your mind about talking to me for the article?" Trace asks, looking down and shuffling her feet.

Leif sighs, "Yeah, but I'll tell you right now, the closer you get, the less you'll get from me."

She opens her mouth to speak, but he cuts her off and says with his hands now moving in his pockets, "Let me just give you the short and skinny. My youngest brother Danton will kill any piece of equipment he can. He's learned probably from watching all his siblings screw up. My oldest sister is a top-shelf bitch. Then there's Dawn . . . she is virtually invisible. Jon is a self-indulgent skinny, closet-alcoholic wiener. Neil is kinda like what you'd expect when you go to the end of the trailer park and you see those dumbbells sitting on someone's deck beside the BBQ. My mother . . . my mother and her husband are a couple of bitchy, tight-ass, thumb-sucking turds. Steph . . . let's just say she's part like Neil and part like her mother . . . kinda like the lady that runs the trailer park. And last but not least, you must've heard about me, this fat bastard pothead. Well, I think I just about covered it. Oh, hang on a second . . . let me add one more person—my dad. The big guy, putting all the dreaming aside and all of the BS that he's had to go through, is still the guy in the family who texts everybody to remind them of birthdays and special occasions."

"Wow, okay, thanks . . ." Trace replies, looking over Leif's shoulder to where Kelly and Odan are conversing. Odan breaks away and returns to where Trace and Leif are standing.

Kelly calls to him, "There's that grey Toyota pickup."

Odan replies, "Call the cops. Better yet, call Brian and get that little drug-dealing Marshall off my property." Odan smiles as he walks toward Trace and Leif.

Trace says, "How many of these houses are you building?"

Kelly's voice from behind blurts out, "We're building eleven . . . too many."

As Odan comes up next to Trace on his way to the truck, he brushes his hand across the small of her back. A frisson passes through her as she turns to follow him. She asks, "What are they made of? I haven't seen any houses like this where I'm from." Leif replies from behind her, "They're made of ICF."

"Insulated concrete forms," Kelly clarifies.

Odan passes by the driver's door and walks to the rear of the truck and looks down in the box. Kelly is looking over at the Toyota truck with two men sitting in it on Odan's vacant lot.

Odan asks, "Kelly, are you planning to take this toolbox out of the back of my truck anytime soon?" He drops the tailgate on his truck and slides the toolbox on top of it. Odan and Kelly unload the toolbox to the side by putting it on a stack of pallets. Kelly grabs a crossbow arrow that is in the back of Odan's truck and turns and looks at the Toyota with a dirty stare. He attempts to conceal the arrow as he walks toward the house.

Trace notices the arrow tip protruding from Kelly's hand and comments, "That your crossbow arrow, Kelly?" Kelly drops the arrow beside his truck and says, "I think I lost this one while shooting out at the farm."

As Trace and Odan climb into the truck, Kelly suddenly calls out, "You going to tap that?"

"Kelly," Odan admonishes as if he disapproves of his crudeness, but he is smiling. "I already have," he responds glibly.

Once in the truck, Trace relaxes and looks over at Odan. "What was that all about?" she asks.

"Kelly will always be Kelly, so you have to remember to take him light-heartedly. He's kind of a dog when it comes to women. But he has a kind heart and he's a good close friend and I'm sure he would do anything for me," Odan states. They both glance down at Ryker then look straight ahead. Odan reaches over and turns the stereo up. Ed Sheeran's "The Castle on the Hill" is just ending.

"I'm getting the idea that you're about as passionate about your music as you are about your automobiles," she says, as she rolls down her window. They round a corner and turn into a small close. Another song by Ed Sheeran, "Photograph," comes on.

Odan nods his head gently and replies, "Maybe a little bit."

They pull in front of a two-tone large brick home and a mature, attractive woman with short blond hair is standing on the porch. Odan stops and opens his door. He climbs out and Ryker shuffles out the driver's side behind him and says, "Dyno, when are you coming back?"

The little boy gets halfway up the sidewalk and turns around and asks it persistently again, "Dyno, when are you coming ba-a-ack?"

"I'm picking you up before school tomorrow," he says.

The little boy goes, "Awww," but continues on his way and both he and the short woman go into the house.

"Do I dare ask?" Trace says.

"Not before two drinks, that's for damn sure," he replies.

As they drive away, Odan's cell phone rings from a blocked number. The voice on the other end says, "She knows where you are now."

"Who is this, and who are you talking about?" he replies sternly.

"You're not in any danger, at least I don't think you are. I'm just letting you know as someone close to you," the voice on the other end continues in a very professional tone.

"I said, who is this?" Odan asks.

Click. The call goes dead.

Trace turns to Odan with a perplexed look and says, "You lead a strange life."

"I've been getting these strange calls lately," he replies. "I don't know what to think of them and because they come from a blocked number, I can't block them myself. I guess I just won't answer anymore . . . but if I don't, I could miss important calls."

The well-dressed man from the airplane is now standing in front of the drugstore looking across at a field of new-construction homes. He's on his cell phone, waiting for it to be picked up on the other end. Janice answers the phone. He says "Are you sitting down?"

She replies, "Yes, I'm sitting down. Where are you?"

He turns his head 180 degrees and says, "I'm in a place called Coldstream," and then after a delay he adds, "and so is she."

"Christ," she replies. "We have to get . . . is there someone there who can cut the string?"

"I'm here, and I do know someone here is tailing me, but that's not where it stops because I think she's got a tag." He adds, "I think she picked it up when she picked up her last go bag."

Janice asks, "Is it one of ours?"

"Bad things!" he replies. He ends the call and puts his cell phone on the passenger seat of the silver Corvette and drives away. His cell records an incoming text, "Cancel Hayden too," illuminating the front seat. He passes by a subdivision, and two men can be seen loading their white trucks at the Odan Harrison Projects construction site. He grabs his cell and takes a picture of them as he passes by.

6

The Guard Comes Down

Trace and Odan are enjoying a bottle of red wine at The Lizard and Chicken. Channi is dressed in a beautiful form-fitting red dress and brings over a second bottle and Odan says, "Don't take the top off just yet. Bring us a couple of Naked Vikings." Channi nods and walks away. Before long, two tall martini glasses with shrimp garnish and strawberries artfully displayed around the base show up. Less than ten minutes later, lobster tails cresting a rare fillet mignon and perfectly groomed stuffed potato with asparagus tips show up at the table.

"Wow!" Trace says.

Odan replies, "Well, it was either this or Skip the Dishes, and every time I order from the Subshop, they seem to get my order wrong. The local Subshop owner is a dick."

She says to him, "Are you ever planning to grow up?"

"Nope . . . I'm just growing out," he replies and looks down.

"You're not fat," she says.

"I wasn't looking at my gut," he quips.

She laughs so hard she has to put down her cutlery. She orders yet another drink after her cocktail. He replies, "As soon as you finish that, we can start this other bottle of wine."

She says, "This martini is really good. Is there any alcohol in it?"

He smiles devilishly and says, "Just a little bit," as he brings up his two fingers and pushes them together by his eyes. Odan looks over at Channi and nods his head, sending her a silent message to bring more drinks. Minutes later, she returns with another Naked Viking. Trace finishes her first glass and hands it to Channi and has a sip of her next one.

"So, I'm here with a pretty lady trying to spill my guts and yet I don't know anything about you, other than your brother is a cop," he says.

She replies, "What's to tell? I went from home to university to marriage to divorce." She rolls an ice cube in her mouth and puts it back in the glass with her left hand.

Taking a chance that the cocktails have kicked in, Odan continues, "Why didn't your marriage work?"

"Really, there's no drama. No kids, just two people drifting apart as they worked on their careers. It's nothing like your story," she adds.

A sombre yet playful tone comes over his voice and he says, "I'm not gonna Nerf this, just so you can have a bunch of flowers and incense for a story. This shit is real and so is my life. It's not perfect. Actually . . ." he says, "fuck it! It is perfect!" He goes on to say, "There's an old expression that everybody's heard, 'Your bed is what you make it.' Well, let's just say I've had a few futons."

She blurts, "What the hell? Your son called me a 'futon.'"

Odan laughs. "Which one?"

She downs her second drink and reaches over and grabs the bottle of wine and uncorks it. She pours herself a couple of ounces and says with a bit of a happy slur, "Your son said it to me not too long ago. Spike."

He leans back in the booth and says, "You're already that close that you're calling Jon, Spike?"

Meanwhile, at the police station, the man from the Corvette is now standing thirty feet away from the booking table and watching as Brian releases Marshall. Brian says to Marshall, "Quit trying to be a big-time drug dealer . . . if you were half the father that you are an asshole, you'd really be something."

Back at The Lizard and Chicken, Trace is getting comfortable. She says with a slight slur, "I've never found men with grey in their beard to be attractive . . . I mean, before you."

With a blush, chuckle and a grin Odan replies, "Two more drinks and I turn into a Chippendale."

She comes back with a giggle and a smile, "They're no fun . . . because they don't take it all off."

"Now who's the funny one here," he says.

"Just trying to keep up with the old guy," she blurts.

"If I take two blue pills, you're gonna need a wheelchair to take you home . . . I mean, I'm gonna need some alone time after that," he states.

She breaks out in laughter. When she's done laughing she says, "What is this all about your son talking about a relationship agreement?"

He strokes his beard with his right hand and says, "Well, years ago, I told him to do it because he had some issues with one of his relationships. And I saw Sheldon do it on *The Big Bang Theory*." Odan finishes stroking his beard, scratches the right side of his cheek and gestures toward the bar with three fingers up. The bartender immediately changes the music.

"What the hell was that?" she says with a little bit more of a slur.

"What do you mean?" he replies.

"You know. I mean . . . you sent a hand signal over to the bar," she explains.

"I just have a playlist that, once in a while, I like to hear when I'm in here and because I own the joint I sometimes get what I want," he replies. The band, The Calling, is now playing as the volume is slightly increased.

Across town, the man in the silver Corvette is following Jeff Marshall's grey Toyota truck, as Marshall drives away from the police station. They drive for a few minutes to the outskirts of town, where Marshall pulls into a parking lot adjacent to a small runway where a small air drone is parked. The man watches as Marshall walks into a small aluminum-frame building.

Trace is stuck in a giggle mode. "You know . . . here's a funny. As a little girl, I used to sneak into the kitchen at night and get a bowl of Cap'n Crunch, and I used to eat it dry. In fact, I ate so much that the roof of my mouth started to get sore and there was, like, a layer of skin that came off."

"I know somebody else who did that, too. Her name is . . . was Kayden. She was an incredible kisser. Maybe the best . . . No, not maybe, she was." He's silent for a moment as he wonders where and how she is. "And now that I think about it," he replies and continues after a pause, "she also drove a Mercedes ragtop. I think she called her car Mona, too".

They're both smiling. Channi stops by the table and he says, "Can you bring me the bill, please?"

Channi smiles and says, "Absolutely. Be right back." She walks away with her country-girl flounce. Elvis Presley's "Can't Help Falling in Love" is now playing through the speakers.

Trace asks, "Can we stay for this? This is one of my favourite songs." "Definitely," he replies as he touches her hand very gently with his fingertips and then pulls it back. He sits up straight and says, giving her a serious look, "I've been guilty more than once of hanging on to a relationship that wasn't there . . . and I've also been on the opposite end of the equation where I should've been straightforward and said I can't do this anymore. Basically, I'm not sure that I ever want to get involved in a relationship where I can't be honest with the other person or myself, and that's it. It gets to a point where both people start believing their own lie. It has nothing to do with friendship and is the furthest thing from love. Sometimes people are just hanging on because it's the most comfortable place to be. They don't know how to communicate or negotiate their feelings."

Trace replies, "I don't know what cavewoman took you to the cleaners, but what I do know is that, personally, I don't give a shit about cards and flowers or any of that crap. What I do care about is the little things, the small gestures."

He stands up slowly beside the table and she rises with him, as he takes a minute to think about exactly what he's going to say. He clears his throat. "I can't sugarcoat this, so I will just say it as clearly as I can. I don't know if I have any romance left in me. I fought off this dark cloud of being seen as a con artist for way too long. My lack of trust . . . just about everything, has gone along with it. I've had to let people go who I love and care about very deeply. Because of my dreams and perception of what was real, it was all taken from me. Starting over should be a term someone uses once or at most twice in their life, but for me, it seems like it's all the time. The hamster wheel in my head tells me to keep on going forward but I think I just need to get off and take a rest and reset. I better get you a cab and call it a night."

She leans into him but he doesn't lean back. She says, "My car is at your house, but I can call a cab from there." He extends his elbow in the shape of a triangle for her to grab on to, which she does. Their eyes lock for a brief moment. The butterflies inside her are flitting in circles. A young man at the door opens it for them and they walk across a half-empty parking lot to his truck. The sound of crickets echoes through the air. The dew is accumulating over the ground and you can feel a warmer day coming.

Odan opens her door for her and she glances back at the restaurant and then she looks at him. She bites her lip and carefully gets in the truck. He takes the seatbelt and swings it over her waist, slowly. His beard gently touches her chin as he leans across her body and they can feel each other's breath for a brief moment. The seatbelt clicks, and he pulls back and waits, pausing inches from her face.

"Really, I'm . . . just a guy trying to get on with my life," he says gently. Then he walks around the truck and gets in and starts it up. He reaches over and turns the stereo off, sits back in the seat and relaxes for a second before he rolls his window down and puts the truck into gear. Every second of the drive back is filled with hot tension. They try to pretend they're not glancing over to analyze each other's faces.

As they pull up to the house, they notice a light on in the turret office room. Looking at her briefly, Odan says, "I'm not sure I left that one on."

"Yeah, I don't think you did," she says, frowning.

As they approach the house, they can hear the neighbours talking around their fire pit down by the water, and a couple of late-night boaters on the lake. Odan unlocks the door and they walk in. "I'll call a ride for you," he states.

She replies quietly as she runs her right hand through her hair, "Thank you. Would you mind if I get a glass of water?"

"Not at all. Help yourself. Look around. Do whatever you want to do. I love the view from the top of the house over the lake. It's actually very nice if you want to go up there." He smiles as he walks toward the open door into the renovated living space that used to be a garage. She smiles gently, slips off her shoes and walks into the kitchen to the right. She says loud enough for him to hear, "Do you mind if I look in your fridge?"

He replies in a playful voice, "Anything you like, darling."

"Did he just say 'darling'?' she whispers to herself. She grabs a bottle of water from a shelf in the two-door fridge. She looks around and whispers again to herself, "He's a damn clean freak."

She quietly looks in the cupboards and notices all matching black-and-grey dishes. She then goes into a drawer and she sees custom grey-and-black silverware. She closes up everything, takes a quick glance around the counter, and walks into the open part of the living room space. On a small ledge eighteen inches off the ground a little money clip sits with hundred dollar bills in it.

Over her shoulder, she says, "I need to ask you a question."

He appears in the doorway and says, "Shoot."

With a smile, raising the bottle as if to cheers, she says, "How can you be so cold?"

"Maybe the fridge was open," Odan states with a slow smile.

"No, really. You know what I mean," she says, and bites her lip.

He takes a second and then says, "It keeps me alive."

"No," she comes back. "It keeps you without me . . . I mean . . . what I meant is . . . . people like me," she stumbles, her voice cracking slightly.

"My life has consisted of . . . making choices that are perilous without knowing they were. I guess I could've led a life of pounding nails like my dad, but my tongue wasn't meant for licking boots," Odan says, stroking the hairs on his chin with his finger.

"What about your books? I hear they're quite intriguing," she says.

"They're just thoughts on paper. Pieces of dreams here and there. Anyone is capable of putting the dark side out there, but not all are capable of controlling the shadows and directing the light," he says calmly.

"Can I quote you on that? That's deep and real," she says.

"Sure. Why not? You can even use it for tonight . . . directly for you. I mean . . . I mean . . . just forget it, you can use it," he says, stumbling over his words.

7

The Break-In

Odan says to Trace, deepening his tone, "You know you're kind of funny but that's for another time. Another time . . ." They both step to face each other and then she turns away.

"Do you mind if I go upstairs and look at the lake while I wait for my ride?" she asks.

"Well, it's gonna be at least twenty minutes, so knock yourself out. Can I grab you anything?" he asks.

"I'm fine," she says and she walks toward the spiral staircase leading to the turret. He walks over to his bedroom on the far left of the living room and stops at the door. She's now at the top of the turret in the office, and she notices there is a desk light on, and the journal is gone. She looks down through the window at the yard terracing down to the lake, and notices a black jet boat with silver stripes at the end of the dock, gently rocking with the evening waves. She looks around, and quickly and quietly walks back down the staircase. They both meet at the pair of leather love seats facing the open patio door to the lake and she sits on one.

With her right hand, Trace plays with the label on the water bottle as she looks down and then up and sees that he's waiting for her to initiate some dialogue. "You have a gorgeous place here and it's very quiet," she states.

"Yeah, it came with a . . . well, let's just say it didn't come without sacrifice," he says.

"But why would you want to live way out here?" she queries. "You're not where the action is, that's for sure."

Odan replies, "No drama. I need those moments. I need the quiet of this place to recharge."

"Everything in here is very tasteful, but it's missing a woman's touch," she says. He sits in the corner of the other love seat. Now they're both within two feet of each other. "You're the one who's writing an article on me, so what have you figured out by now?" he asks, cracking a gentle smile.

"You're not the big bad villain that some say you are," she says.

He reaches down between them to a little circular table not more than eight inches in diameter and picks up a half-empty coffee cup and studies the contents as if they contain some kind of secrets. "There were women. Kayden, Loraine, Emily and Hope. They got to me. They weren't the only ones."

After a delay, she says quietly, gazing out over the lake. "Gwen gave me a lot of information. Will you let me try to put the pieces of the puzzle together?"

"Gwen's known me for a long time. In fact, a very long time, and her and her husband have hearts of gold. Al is one of those guys who if he had his own machine shop, could fabricate anything. Gwen, on the other hand, is as sweet as the day is long. She can grow anything and she is just such a down-to-earth country girl that I—" There's a pause. He looks down and sinks back into the seat.

Trace says, "You didn't finish . . . 'that I . . . what'?"

"Good people. They're just good people. And the same can be said for Kelly and Robert."

Trace puts the water bottle down on the floor and turns to look him in the eye. Then she says, "Gwen gave me the letter you wrote some time ago where you talk about what you want in a woman."

"What the hell!?What would she do that for?" he says, then he chuckles. "I guess she thought that would be an easy way for you to try understand who I am."

He adjusts his shirt and smiles then says, "Some of that shit in there is real and some of that stuff . . . I was just venting. Some of that stuff—the grandmother stuff in there—I wouldn't want anyone to read that, but it's all true. Ryker has a grandmother full of hate and the ability to be a not-so-nice person."

Trace sits up straight and says, "I don't remember there being anything about grandmothers in that letter."

"Well, I'm good, then. You must not have the revised version," he concludes.

She picks up the bottle of water and has a slow drink. She asks in a curious tone, "There's a revised version?"

"Oh, yeah. It talks a lot about Ryker," he says quietly.

"I don't know if I should ask what the story there is," she states.

"There is no story," he replies. "I have him because I believe it's the best place for him to be. His father is no longer with us, and his two grandmothers are in a place . . .

well, I don't feel comfortable explaining it because of the circumstances."

Odan lowers his head and continues, "He's a shy but energetic little guy who deserves better than what life has given him. It's simple. I'm not giving up on him, and that's the best thing for him, so . . . if I have to make sacrifices in my personal life, so be it. I was a shitty husband. God knows if I could go back in time, I'd try to fix things. But that's not the way it is in the real world. I'm sure my kids wish I was the father that I am now to this little guy, but I can't change the past."

He brings his hands to the inside of his knees then raises his right index finger to rub the corner of his eye, and continues on, "I'm going to make the best of it, no matter what. From here on out, I'm always going to be me."

"You have a very colourful past," she states, after a moment's hesitation.

Odan raises his head and says, "You're a woman. After a bad relationship, women can turn vindictive and spiteful, and as my eldest son would say, some can be top-shelf bitches. Even if they start a new relationship themselves, the vast majority of them do not want to see their ex in a healthy relationship . . . screw that, I meant to say they don't want to see them happy. In fact, I asked a woman once if she ever shed a tear, looking at the place where I used to sleep." He stands up and walks toward the glass doors facing the lake and then turns back around. "I've never met my real parents."

Trace asks him softly, "Have you ever tried to find your biological parents?"

He takes a few steps away from her then comes back and puts his left hand on the love seat behind her left shoulder and bends over and whispers in her ear, "Many times, but I'm not getting hurt again."

He stands upright and puts the coffee cup down on another table and once again puts his hands in his front pockets. He turns to her and says, "You are one of the prettiest girls I've seen in a very, very long time . . . or, should I say, woman. I have let more than one woman go in the past, and many have let me go. A relationship is a big investment and I don't think—no, I *guarantee* I don't have what it takes to invest in one again."

A quiet smile comes over her face.

He says, "I hope you'll excuse me. I just have to run and get something out of the bedroom and it's getting late. Your cab should be here soon."

She stands up and says, "Wait." She walks over to him and stops in front of him, slowly reaching up and giving him a kiss on his left cheek. She feels a warm rush but does not know what he feels. Odan returns her gaze, his eyes searching her face. He then touches her gently on her left hip. He surrenders a small smile but then turns away and walks into his bedroom. Three minutes pass.

Odan comes running out of his bedroom on his cell phone, saying, "Yeah, I'd like to report a break-in. It's 117 Kuusamo, off the Rainy Creek Road." Just then, they both hear, through the open back door, a V8 jet boat race away, bouncing off the white crest of the waves.

He looks at Trace and he says, "I'm just going to have a look around." He grabs her gently by both shoulders. "Just don't go too far." There's a flashlight on the shelf. He

grabs it as he hurries out through door. She can see the
beam from the flashlight combing the surrounding area,
and the scurrying of a scared little quail as it darts out of
the bush. An eerie sense comes over her. Her mind jumps
to the diary. She looks around and tries to decide what to
do or where to go. She walks toward the love seat and sits
back down, bringing her knees up and resting the water
bottle on top of them. He comes back in and gives her an
assertive, quick smile before he goes up the staircase to
the turret. She can hear his footsteps pacing around in his
office and sees the lights come on. Then he comes down
the staircase with a heavy step and slows. He turns left
and goes through the kitchen, then he's out of view for a
moment. She can still hear the neighbours down by their
campfire as if nothing has happened.

Two police cars show up in the driveway. Their top
lights are not on. The front doors open and a tall, slender
male officer walks through the door. He looks at Trace
sitting on the love seat and asks in a professional tone, "Is
everybody okay here?"

Trace stands up and turns around to face him. She
says in a rattled tone, "I'm not sure. He's—he's—he's right
there," she says, pointing to Odan, as he comes closer.

"Hi, Officer. Somebody's been in my home but I can't
find anything taken . . . yet. I haven't really had a chance to
look around much."

Trace is puzzled because she thought that perhaps his
journal had been taken, but then she wonders if it has just
been placed elsewhere. She has no intention of bringing it
up because she doesn't feel it's her place.

The policeman states, "Do you mind if I take a few notes?" He starts walking toward the opening to the kitchen, then turns back to look to Odan for permission.

Odan replies, "Feel free to look around, but I'm not sure anything has been touched. It's kind of like somebody was just snooping."

The officer walks through the home and notices the expensive watches, the money clip and other items he thinks should've been taken if this was a robbery. Then Brian passes through the doorway, accompanied by a heavy-set female officer. The first thing that comes out of his mouth is, "Trace, why are you here? Or do I dare ask?"

Odan quickly and sarcastically responds, "I called a driver to take her home, but I didn't know I was talking to Mickey Mouse Uber." He and Brian lock eyes for a moment and Odan gives him a condescending smile.

The female officer says quietly to herself, "Great! Robin fuckin' Williams wannabe just got robbed."

Odan says quickly, "I heard that. Chuck E. Cheese isn't far," staring directly at the heavy-set female cop.

Trace pipes up with her hands on her hips, "What's going on here?"

Brian says, "Let's just say it's a friendly rivalry."

The female officer looks up and past everybody at the lake through the patio doors and says, "Let's just get done and get back to the donut shop. Right, O-o-o-dan?"

Brian and Trace walk into the converted garage as the officers and Odan separate and go into different rooms. Brian walks halfway through the opening and gets within ten feet of the pool table.

He turns sideways, purposely facing away from Trace and ask her, "What's really going on here?"

"It's not what you think. I'm not jumping him. It was simple. We had plans to go for supper and have a talk and here we are. I've already called a driver to take me home, and he has been a perfect gentleman. He's kind of goofy, that's for sure, and he commands his own space, but he's a good guy, Brian."

Trace walks away from Brian; she stops and leans on the pool table. Walking around it slowly, she grabs a cue from underneath the table. She lines up her shot, takes a difficult shot at the seven ball and it rolls across the table toward the eight ball, which is resting near a corner pocket. The ball rolls up and comes to rest at the edge of the pocket, only to be stopped by a yellow pencil which is in the pocket. She walks over and pulls the pencil out and the eight ball falls into the pocket. She places the cue on the pool table. Then she walks over to a table that's pushed up against the wall and looks up.

"Those are pictures from Odan's past. All those people you see are people he thought were his friends and they all betrayed him in one way or another. The pictures you see on the right are his exes," Brian says to her speaking from twenty feet away, holding a picture behind his back that he snuck off the wall while she was lining up her shot.

Trace replies with curiosity, "There's a space here. There's a picture missing." Trace carefully looks at the pictures, trying to absorb the smallest of details, while her brother remains frozen in the archway, debating how best to make his exit without her seeing the photograph he is holding.

Miss Guided

Brian says, "You can do what you want to do. You're a big girl, but I'm telling you this could be trouble."

With a scolding face she replies, "You are the damn cop here. What just happened? Who ransacks somebody's house and takes nothing, including a stack of hundred dollar bills lying over there on the shelf by the fireplace?" She points toward to the fireplace with one hand and runs her other hand through her hair.

He replies, "I'm not sure."

"Listen, you may be my brother, and I do love you. I'm here, back in town. I'm doing a story on a guy, and there are cops at the door. Explain that to me, Sherlock," Trace growls.

Fifteen hundred miles away, Janice gets a phone call. She sits up in her bed and answers it with her left hand, using her right hand to brush her hair from her face. "What!? You're kidding me! When did it happen? How much did she get?" She puts her phone on her lap and reaches over with her other hand and turns on the modern lamp beside her. She pauses for a second and cancels the call. Then she pushes back the covers to reveal another woman lying beside her and gets up and walks toward the window. She pushes a number on speed dial. She looks down on her large front yard that has five flood lights surrounding a fifteen-foot-tall water fountain and a red Porsche convertible parked beside it, half in the shadows.

She says into the phone, "She just knocked out our computers! She's managed to grab two hundred and fifty million dollars of our money!" Lowering her frantic tone, she continues, "All our go bags on the West Coast are missing. I used to think of her as a kite—you know, one of those assets where you can just cut the string and all liabilities are gone. Get the money and just take her down."

The voice on the other end says after a delay, "Fifteen, Grand Caymans."

Janice pauses for a second and says, "Ten . . . when the job's done." She cancels the call and tosses the cell on the bed.

Back at Odan's house, the three police officers converge in the living room by the entrance to the master bedroom.

The female officer says to the other two, "We heard about the boat but it could have belonged to a resident."

The tall officer replies, "I went over and talked to the neighbours and they've got nothing to say. It's like somebody slipped in and slipped out."

Brian separates from the two officers and casually walks over to his sister. "I cancelled your ride home. I'm gonna take you home myself."

She replies, "That's okay, but, I have to say good night to Odan first." She looks around and sees him standing on the deck, staring out across the lake, leaning on the two-by-four railing. Brian says, "I'll see you in the car" and turns and walks away. She walks into the kitchen and puts the empty bottle of water down beside the sink. She passes through the kitchen and to the other side, crossing her arms and walking out the opening onto the deck. She can hear the quiet voices of his neighbours as they wrap up their fire pit gathering. The waves are gently crashing against the shoreline. In the quiet hush, she comes to stand beside him. "That's more exciting than any night I've had in the big city in fifteen years . . . I feel bad for you. I just want to say, thank you for the evening."

"Why should you feel bad for me? It was just a bit of a rough ending to an otherwise pretty kick-ass night," he replies with a straight, honest face, while still looking forward.

She twists a little bit at the torso and says, "Well, I still had fun . . . other than my brother taking me home in a police car," and smiles.

"I can imagine other ways I'd rather end a night with a beautiful woman," he says with a cautious face.

"You think I'm beautiful," she replies softly, biting her lip slowly.

"Life's . . . it's kind of like a journey down a gravel road . . . always under construction. At least it has been for me . . . and I'm too damn old for this kind of stuff. I've made so many mistakes in my life and most of them have been due to not being honest about when it's time to say goodbye," he says. He takes his hands, pushes them into his front pockets and turns to her gently. "Would you like to go with me on a little road trip tomorrow?"

Sobering up, a warm sensation of anticipation curling in her stomach, she replies, "I think I'd like that, but on that note . . . I have an officer waiting for me out front." She looks up at him with a smile.

He pulls his right hand out of his pocket and moves it to shake her hand, his palm facing up. "Meet me at my office at nine," he says.

She places her hand in his and gently weighs it downward, then they slowly pull apart. She turns and walks away through the kitchen and across the house, not looking back until she's almost out the front door. She sees him standing in the kitchen and rolls her fingers in a goodbye gesture and smiles briefly. He returns her smile and when she's gone, his face turns sad. He turns and takes heavy steps back through the house, taking a seat outside on the patio. He places his elbows on his knees and runs his hands through his hair, then rests his chin on his knuckles. He looks out over the lake and a tear escapes from his right eye.

An overwhelming tiredness comes over Trace, as she rides back along the curvy road with her brother in his unmarked SUV. The picture Brian took from Odan's house is rattling in its frame underneath Brian's seat. They both hear it but he attempts to distract her from asking about it. "So, where did you guys go tonight?" he asks her.

Assertively, she states, "I am not your fucking prisoner here for questioning, but if you really wanna know . . . we went to a construction site for a bit. Then he dropped off the little boy he takes care of. Then we went to The Lizard and the Chicken for cocktails and some great food. It was a lot of fun. He's more than a one-colour guy, you know." After a moment's hesitation, she continues, "He has an ability to turn the switch on and be one person and then, in a blink of an eye, he's another. He's got a vulnerable side. I just don't know what the deal around that little boy is."

Trace's cell phone rings and displays "Odan Harrison Projects."

"Who would be calling me at this hour?" she says. "Hello?" she answers slowly. The voice on the other end asks, "Are you okay?"

"Who is this?" she asks.

"This is Leif. My father called me and told me what happened."

"It's so kind of you to call," she replies.

"I get my nice side from my dad. I hear you're meeting with him again tomorrow." She pauses, looking at Brian. "Yeah, I guess. I'm meeting him at his office at nine. Why do you ask?"

He answers, "I thought we could grab a coffee before you go out there."

Confused, she answers, "Yeah, okay."

"How about the Rugged Bean on the corner of 111th and 23rd at 8:15?" he asks. She replies, "I can make that happen."

"Once again, I'm happy nothing happened to you," Leif replies.

"I'm fine. I think your dad is going over the house to see what they might have taken, if anything."

He replies, "My dad is pretty anal retentive, so if anything is missing, he'll be able to figure it out." He asks again, "And are you sure you're able to meet with me in the morning?"

She replies, "It's no problem, really. See you then."

When she gets off her phone, Brian asks her, "How are you planning to get there since your car is back at Odan's?"

"I'm sure I can borrow Dad's truck," she replies, "or . . . can you give me a ride out there in the morning?"

He twists his grip on the steering wheel and says calmly, "What the hell. I have to go out there anyway so I can finish this report in the daylight when I can see."

"Thanks again, bro. I'm sorry for being such a bitch," she says as the vehicle's tires roll to a stop, crunching the gravel on the laneway in front of her parents' house. She tell him goodnight and he waits until he sees her light come on in her bedroom. As he brother drives away, her heart and her mind are engaged in an awkward tango. Once in bed, she runs the fingers of her right hand down the inside of her thigh and fights off the building craving to pleasure herself.

The next morning, just after 7:30 a.m., Trace hears, "Wake up, wake up!"

Her brother stands over her bed, dressed in a golf shirt, running shoes and a pair of grey slacks and explains, "We have to get a move on, so you got to get your crap together."

She sits up. "Yeah, yeah, yeah. I'll be down in three minutes. Does anybody sleep in around here?"

Brian walks out the door and says, "That's what you get for being a night owl." He closes the door and she slowly makes her way to the bathroom. She flicks her hair back with her right hand and faces the mirror.

She says to herself, "Well, big guy, what surprises do you have for me today?" She reaches over and turns on the shower. Ten minutes later, she comes downstairs with wet hair, wearing a short-sleeved teal blouse, a short grey skirt, an ankle bracelet on her left ankle, and a pair of white Under Armour running shoes.

Her father passes in front of her at the base of the stairs with a coffee cup in his hand. "Nothing exciting ever happens in this town, and then you show up." He smiles and adds, "It's a nice day out there."

She says to her father, "Did I hear some sarcasm there?"

"Not at all," he replies. He turns and smiles and looks right at her, "But it's kind of the truth. We've had nothing exciting happen in this town for a very long time."

"I'm just writing a story, Dad," she attempts to assure him.

"Yeah . . . every morning, the weatherman tells a story but I never get excited to hear what he did last night."

Trace and Brian leave out the door. Trace looks behind her and she sees her dad grinning after them. As they get into Brian's SUV, he says, "Beautiful day."

She gets in, and as she is buckling her seatbelt, she looks over at Brian and says, "What's the skinny in regards to your casual attire this morning? I haven't seen you wear sneakers . . . ever."

He replies, "I have to stop by the track today and do a short fitness test. They're making big changes at the department."

Trace states, "I'm not sure that female officer from last night is going to make the cut." She smiles, looking over at Brian.

"Yeah, she's going to start training and has no opportunity for advancement until she can pass the exam. She's one of our best, though. She's got a great mind."

"What's up between her and Odan?" she asks.

"Personally, I think he has some admiration for her, unlike some of the other officers at the force," he states. As they drive, the police radio comes on and a voice says, "Donna hasn't shown up for work today."

Brian picks up the CB and says, "No worries. She's probably taking a sick day. If you just wait a bit, she'll probably check in."

The voice on the other end says, "Copy." Then they continue, "That Toyota is back on Odan's construction site. It was reported late last night."

"What time did the report actually come in?" Brian asks.

"Let me just check," the voice says. "It looks like it came in while you were out at Kuusamo last night."

Brian replies, "I'll swing by there on my way back to the office, probably in an hour or so. Have an officer meet me out there with the tow truck just in case."

"Copy that."

A look that could kill comes over Trace. Brian drops her off at her car. She gets out and says to Brian, "I'll see you a little bit later."

He replies back, "Why the hell are you giving me the death stare?"

"You know why," she replies.

With a smile, he leans over on the seat. "Have a good day."

She walks by her car and passes Odan's black truck and decides to walk past the deck. She comes around the corner and sees Odan sitting on the patio chair, wearing a headset and talking on his phone. Their eyes meet and he smiles and nods his head then continues on with his conversation. He's got a coffee cup sitting beside him with a picture of Ryker printed on it, and as he gestures with his hands, she sees a bright red pen in his left hand.

There's a pause and he says to whomever he is speaking with, "We'll do a flyover at thirteen hundred hours." Then he ends the call with a "thank you." He pulls off his headset and smiles at her and stands up. "I wasn't expecting you this early." He comes down and gives her a gentle hug.

"My brother roused me out of bed and that's okay because apparently I'm having coffee with your son this morning," she states. "You and I are still on for nine o'clock, aren't we?" he asks.

"Definitely," she answers. As he walks her to her car, he places his right hand on the small of her back. She actually slows down just so she can feel the pressure of his hand.

Just miles away, the Tour Guide, dressed in tight-fitting jeans and a black Stepchild tank top with her blond hair hanging over her face, sits at a table in a small dark pub texting, "I want to mod the car. I need the engine swap done. I want that Cleveland out and the Coyote with the Whipple in. You know, have Billington's boys stripe my truck. Have him redo my boat, too. The Park knows how I want it. Tell Edward I need his tattooing gear . . .

twenty boxes of zip ties . . . fifteen cases of Monk red wine, from Ashley. I need two thousand milligrams of Sublinox. Better yet make it three from White. Have Chuckles drop it off at the mano . . . I'll be there in twenty minutes Seventy kilograms of slow burn from Cody, which I'll pick up in five."

She looks away, and presses End on her cell. She grabs her pint of dark ale and downs it. A call comes in just as she puts the glass down. She slides the glass across the uneven wood table.

"I was wondering when you were going to call."

A male voice says. "You're taking the whole thing down—you don't give a shit about the collateral damage—and I'm going to be there to watch."

The Tour Guide says calmly, "The stain is now not only on my bad days but on my good days, too, and I'm just doing what I should have done many years ago. Couldn't get the stains out so it's time to get rid of it. And if it ever gets to that . . . please tell him I'm sorry." She ends the call and walks out of the restaurant.

9

Bad Things

Odan and Trace walk across the yard back to her vehicle. The tension is thick between them. He lets his left hand trail over the mirror on her driver's side door. She opens the door and climbs in. He backs up as she buckles her seatbelt and rolls her window down so she can speak. She reaches over and turns down the volume on her stereo, then glances up at Odan.

"So, I'll see you after I have a coffee with your son?"

He runs his hand across the window sill. "If—and that's a big *if*—you can make it before nine, that would be great," he replies.

"I'll do my best," she tells him, smiling, and backs down the driveway. At the turn, she wiggles her fingers and calls out, "Should I be worried? I don't know what I'm getting into!"

Rocking back on his heels, his hands in his pockets, he replies, "It's just a story, right?"

She puts the car in Drive and pulls away, looking in the mirror the whole time. He stands there until she's out of view. She drives back to Mason with her hair bouncing around in the early morning breeze. She's imagining a brief kiss as he goes off to work. Her cell rings and she pushes Accept. The voice on the other end says, "Are we still on?"

She replies, "Yes, Leif, we're still on. While I've got you on the phone, can I ask you a question?"

He replies, "Don't say that. My dad has given me shit over the years for starting off a question by asking 'Can I ask you a question?' What's up?

"Has your dad ever been in love?" she questions.

"Oh shit, that's loaded. Dad said you're a cut-to-the-chase kind of girl but I thought he was kidding," he replies. Then he continues, "Why, after just a couple of days of knowing me, would you ask a question like that? But to know my dad, you must know the good, the bad and the ugly. Pick a number. If I was a girl, I would run as far away as I could from my dad. As a guy, or a business guy, I want to get as close as I can get to learn every secret he knows."

Just then a call comes in for Trace. She says, "I got to go. I'll see you there." She hangs up and clicks on the other call.

"Trace, are you there? Brian here. You're not gonna believe this shit, but a tow truck driver just showed up at one of Odan's sites, and they found a small-time drug dealer in the back of his truck with forty-one needles in him. Half of his blood was on the front seat and he had a twenty-inch crossbow arrow sticking out his mouth. Maybe it's time to pull back from the story until we get things figured out. He was known to have a lot of friction with the big guy. His name was Jeff Marshall."

Trace asks, "What exactly does this have to do with Odan?"

"Marshall was a small-time thug. But that's the opinion of others, not mine. He used the big guy's property for meetings. No one knows for sure, but one thing I do know is that he slammed the big guy a lot. I know you're my sister, but if you've got anything you want to share, now is the time."

Trace replies, "You know I was with him last night, and when this call came through the radio, I saw the whites of your eyes."

Brian replies, "My eyes may have been white but last night yours were looking a little bloodshot."

She says to her brother, "I've got a job to do . . . so why don't I do mine, and you do yours? I got the transcripts from Odan's court cases, and a list of names."

"These hard feelings and this animosity have been going on for a long time. I just wish you wouldn't get involved . . . Please, sis, stop this shit before it gets real."

Before she hangs up she says, "I love you, but do your job."

Another call comes through on her cell. The name and number are blocked. She reluctantly answers and says, "Hello."

The voice on the other end is female She doesn't recognize it, but the caller sounds like she could possibly be of South African descent. She says simply, "You need to back off."

Trace replies, "I don't know who you are. I don't know who you work for. I don't know what this pertains to, but, let me tell you, the fact that you called me and told me what to do really pisses me off."

After a delay the voice says, "People involved in this are going to die. If you stay away from the target, you won't get hit."

Trace replies, "If you won't tell me who you are, I'll take you for what you are, just another cog in the wheel."

The voice says, "You dug her up and now everybody's got to pay."

With a puzzled and annoyed look on her face, Trace elevates her voice and asks, "If you don't tell me who you are and what this is all about before I push End on this fucking phone, I will pretend you never existed, you dizzy bitch."

There's another delay and finally the voice says, "My name is Margot. I'm trying to stop someone very bad from doing very bad things."

"Okay, Margot. Please enlighten me, because I have no idea what you're talking about."

Margot replies in her South African accent, "It's kind of like putting your false teeth in your back pocket. You know they're there and you know eventually you're going to get bit in the ass." She adds, "Trust me, this woman is someone you don't want to cross swords with."

Bewildered, Trace says, "Why are we talking about a woman? I am doing an article on a retired or semi-retired inventor."

The phone goes *click*. As Trace pulls into the coffee shop, she notices that there are three men and a woman standing outside. She gets out of her car and is focusing on the people as she walks toward the door. She overhears one of the men say, "Did you hear about that drug dealer?" She walks through the door, and the large redheaded man,

Odan's son, waves at her. He gestures at a table with his left hand at the coffees that are already resting on the table.

She gets within five feet and he says, "I don't know how you take it, so it's just a coffee."

She replies, "Thanks so much. I'll be right back," and she walks over to the service table where the milk and cream are. The coffee shop is starting to pack up with a line of people extending almost past the door. She mixes in a packet of cream and walks quickly back to the table and sits down.

"So, is this your favourite hangout?" she asks.

"Not at all. This is way too damn expensive for me," he replies. Then he continues, "I knew you were on your way to see my dad, and this is fairly close. My brother has started coming here because he calls this place 'Cougars 'R' Us.'"

"May I ask why you wanted to have this coffee? I really don't have any major questions for you," she states.

"I just thought you were shook up after what happened last night," he replies.

She asks him, "Have you heard what happened at your father's construction site?"

With a surprise look on his face, he replies as he picks up his coffee to take a sip, "I didn't know it was at my dad's place. I just heard that someone got killed."

"Yeah, it happened sometime late last night. I guess we'll probably hear more about it today," she says. She twists off the lid on the coffee cup and takes a little stir stick and scrapes it around the edge. "Well, while I'm here, what do I really want to know?"

Leif leans back in his chair and asks, "Is this about our family, or is this about my dad?" He takes his left foot and rests it on the base of the table and the table moves ever so slightly. He looks down as a little coffee has spilled over the top of Trace's cup and surrounded the base. "Oops, I'm sorry," he states.

She takes a moment. She doesn't reply. She picks up a napkin and circles the cup but doesn't lift it. "What can you tell me about your dad's journal?" she asks.

"WYD? 'Wish You Dead' as us kids call it. There's not much to tell. No one knows what's in it. He keeps it close at all times and he writes in it very frequently. I think eighty percent of it is just full of aircraft talk, notes for himself, possibly a wish list. Why do you ask?" he says, as his eyes become interested.

She takes her time. She glances up at him and then out the window, then back at him again. With a casual smile, she says, "I don't know. There's something about that journal . . . because I saw it in one place before we went out for supper and then when we got back, it wasn't there. It kind of disappeared. I mean, I think that whoever was in the house took it."

"I wouldn't worry about it. Did my dad mention it at all?" Leif asks.

"No . . . it's just an observation. I'm probably imagining things." She finally takes a drink of coffee. "Does every line your brother uses come from your dad?"

"Of course. If you asked my dad about Starbucks twenty five years ago, my dad would have said it's a better cut of meat," Leif says candidly.

Trace slides the napkin under the base of her cup. As she brings the cup to her mouth she asks, "So...is Spike's taking over where your dad left off ...or has your dad just grown up?"

There's silence as Leif doesn't reply.

"I'm still confused about why you called me. Is there something you want to get off your chest?" she asks.

"Not really. Things have been tense lately and usually bad things come in bunches for my dad. Quite frankly, a lot of them have to do with women." He stares at her for a bit and she looks away as if trying to plan her next move.

A somewhat jolly smile comes over him and he says to her, "I'm kind of surprised if you really wanna know the truth."

She leans forward and asks, "What's the truth?"

He mimics her pose and says to her in a polite, familiar tone, "You went out with my dad, you left your car at his place, the police took you home, and now you're going to see him again. Doesn't that sound kinda messed up? You could've written the story already by now, but you're gonna see him again."

She states, "I'm not finished. There's more here, I know, and I will treat him fairly, I promise."

"Well, I got to go to work before my dad skids me," Leif says.

"Thanks for the coffee," she replies.

They stand up and he waits for her to go first. She gets into her car and when she's seated behind the steering wheel, she notices a folded piece of paper under the windshield wiper. She gets out of her car and looks around.

Puzzled, she removes it and she gets back in her car. She sits and unfolds the small piece of paper.

The paper says, "Back here at 11:30 TG," in distinct slanted script. She folds it up and puts it in the centre console then she pulls out of the parking lot. She accelerates as she pulls out onto the main road because heavy traffic is coming up on her. She has only five miles to go and she decides to push her car. A black Challenger goes whistling past her in the fast lane. She tightens her left hand on the steering wheel and nails the gas pedal to the floor. She passes the Dodge. She's doing one hundred miles an hour now. She pulls off on the panel so she can make the next exit to the airport.

Meanwhile, Brian is with a group of officers going over the Marshall crime scene. The body is being taken away by the coroner. Brian asks the lead officer, "So, what are the details?" The lead officer is the tall gentleman who he was with the night before, out at Kuusamo. The officer replies, "All the needles that were in his body and the combination of acid—we'll have to wait until we get the tox report back from the coroner." He continues, "But the strange thing is, he was shot in the back of the neck with an arrow first, and then it's as if he was dragged around the inside of his vehicle without any signs of a struggle. The keys are in the ignition. It's got a full tank of gas. The car was taken through a car wash recently, just the exterior. Time of death was shortly after we left Odan's house last night."

"I'm gonna tell you right now, looking at it this, it looks like it was a pro hit. Somebody is sending a message and I'll bet there's more coming," Brian answers sharply.

The officer holds up his hand. "There is more, Boss. I just got notified that, across town, an insurance guy, Rob Chant, was found crushed inside his Nissan Murano at an auto wrecker with the same type of twenty-inch crossbow arrow through his neck, and a truck driver originally from Romania was found partially eaten . . . by what, we don't know yet. He was found in his Kenworth, covered in feces . . . same MO—an arrow through his torso, protruding through his genitals."

The men part and walk away. Brian walks back to his SUV. He gets a call. "You're supposed to be picking up those papers from the courthouse in an hour, just a reminder," says the friendly voice on the other end.

Brian says, "Yeah, I'll try to make it as quick as possible, but I've got to swing by and do twenty-five minutes' worth of that fitness exam at Tower Track."

"Yes, I know you and three other officers are slated to be there today," the voice says.

"It's going to be okay. I'm sure one of us is going to pass. I guess my days of stuffing my face at Rotten Ronnie's are numbered," says Brian.

The voice on the other end says, "The chances of that happening are slim to none. I've seen you eat . . . but that doesn't mean we can't pretend."

Brian replies, "Even cops need a cheat day."

The voice says, "That's why they call it a cheat day and not a cheat month. Ten-four out"

Brian pulls up to Tower Track, which is a football field. It has grandstands on one side. It's getting warmer by the minute. A warm breeze blows across the field from the south. Brian gets out of his SUV and puts his cell phone on the passenger seat. It's about a hundred and fifty feet to the gate that leads into the track. Just before he reaches the entrance, a quail runs in front of him into the long grass by the fence. He sees a Black man dressed in a T-shirt and shorts and two other individuals with their backs turned to him. Ten feet on the other side of the group is a chin-up bar and nine coloured boxes of various heights. The people standing on the field all turn around and their faces brighten.

"I'm coming in!" Brian smiles. "This is going to be an easy one."

"Hi, Brian," the trainer chirps.

"Hello, Ryan," Brian replies. "How did you pull off this gig?"

"I was offered the job over a year ago. I just never took them up on it until I could do it here in my hometown," Ryan replies. "I thought I couldn't have picked a better job to get out of my unpaid tickets, but now I see you guys and I'm feeling like I'm probably going the wrong way in that department," he says, grinning.

Brian asks, "Aren't there supposed to be four of us?"

Ryan looks down at his clipboard and says, "Yes, there is supposed to be one female officer here today, too."

"We only have eight female officers at the department, so which one of them didn't show up?" Brian says, then a serious expression comes over his face. "Oh . . . Donna."

Ryan turns and says, "Well, we can't wait for her. Come with me. Here's where we start up and down the grandstand stairs twenty times." He holds up a stopwatch in his right hand and clicks it. "You're on the clock, guys."

The three men start up the stairs. They are talking, but Ryan can't quite make out what's being said. He starts barking, "Pick up the pace, guys. I haven't got all day!"

Trace pulls into the parking lot at the airport. The extremely large Mi-26 helicopter is on the tarmac. The one-hundred-and-five-foot rotors are spinning and the bend is coming out of them. She drives through to the parking lot beside the hangar. Two white Ford pickup trucks and Odan's little black-and-silver truck are outside. The big hangar scissor-bifold doors are open. Half a dozen men scramble. The small twin-engine P-68 with the glass nose is being towed out of the hangar.

Odan comes down the stairs and walks briskly toward her. She reaches in her pocket and pulls out a bright red hair scrunchie and twists it in her hair as she approaches him. He greets her with a grand smile on his face. "Good, you're gonna need that. We're going to go flying today."

"Do I need to grab anything from my car?"

"Do you have sunglasses? You may need them today."

"Yes, I do in the car," she replies.

"Well, maybe you should run and grab them quickly before we go. This will just be a quick flight. We're going to go check a few campgrounds and a cutline outside of town, about seventy five miles from here."

A couple of men walk over and he introduces them. "Trace, this is Jeff Hammond and Tom Couture, chief pilot and PRM. They're going to be flying the plane today. You and I are going to be in the back, running the infrared camera."

The men say, almost in unison, "Nice to meet you."

"I'm just going to grab my sunglasses from the car," Trace says to them and jogs back to the parking lot. Odan can't help but to watch her run. He tilts his head, and puts on his sunglasses . . . and smiles.

The pilots board the plane and drive it over to a small fuelling station. Trace returns, wearing her glasses and Odan guides her over to the plane. The small door on the left-hand side under the window is open and the pilots are in their position up at the front.

Odan says to her with a smile, "You'll have to put your cell phone on vibrate." She climbs through the small door and turns left inside the airplane fuselage and sits down where he's pointing. He climbs in and fastens her seatbelt around her waist for her. He checks the tension on the belt and when she looks up at him, their eyes are less than ten inches apart and they both smile.

He gives her a headset and he sits down. Odan does up his belt, pushes the seat back and swings down the monitor in front of him. He pulls the microphone away from his mouth and says to her, "You can hear everything, but when you push the button to talk . . . you only talk to me. Try it now."

She does as he says, trying to speak over the sound of the aircraft.

"Good enough," he says. "That works for me. After you're finished talking, just try to say 'clear' or 'copy,'" he adds.

The left engine fires first and then the right. A small puff of smoke comes out of the engine on Trace's side. After a minute of the engines revving up, the pilot says into the headset, "Mrs. Scott, are you ready for this?"

"It's Ms . . . and yes, copy," she replies.

The co-pilot's voice comes over the radio, "I'm gonna fly at eighteen hundred AGL, going north on location, then taking a swing back and following the burn line around the city back to here, correct?"

"Affirmative," says Odan. The small plane taxis down the runway and swings left and throws the sun under its wings. The break goes on the plane. Trace can hear the pilot talk clearly and broadcast to the tower, "This is Charlie, Foxtrot, Lima, India, Romeo, requesting take off on three, four."

The voice comes back, "Clear."

The small plane accelerates and the Lycoming engines start to whine as the plane lifts off the ground. Odan looks down and then across the floor. On the left side of the monitor, he can see a bruise on the inside of Trace's left thigh. He also notices her ankle bracelet. The bracelet is dancing with the vibration of the plane. She looks out the window to her right and he peeks his head out from behind the monitor and catches a glimpse of her white panties and chooses to bring his face back behind the monitor before he speaks.

He says, "We're gonna be gone for a couple hours, so relax and we'll try to make some money."

She says, "What time do you think we'll be back?"

He pushes the monitor aside for a second and says, "It all depends on our patrol."

The pilot calls out, "We are now at eighteen AGL and panning right."

Odan adjusts the joy stick and moves the gimbal. The pilot and co-pilot are talking back and forth, giving coordinates, which Trace can see them plug in on the monitor.

Trace says, "This is beautiful!" Gazing outside, she carries on, "Is there a chance that we could swing by my place so I can take a picture of my parents' house from here?"

The pilot comes back on the radio, "It's totally up to the big guy. It's his plane." Another plane radios in and there is silence for a second and then the co-pilot gets on the radio and replies, "Ray, can you fly at low, just over the crest of the hill behind us?" Trace asks, "What is that?"

Odan replies, looking straight at her, "That's Ray. He's flying a BD Cessna 337." "What does that mean?" she asks.

"BD means bird-dog. Cessna is the manufacturer and 337 is the plane type. It's also called a 'huff-puff' or a 'push-pull'. Remind me to show you when we get on the ground," he says.

She looks out the window but she's also thinking of that piece of paper that she found on her windshield wiper. Whoever put it there and whatever it meant, she won't be there to find out.

It's eleven-thirty in the morning and the temperature is already approaching ninety. Brian walks to his SUV, exhausted, finished with his fitness test. The sweat runs off all the men as they walk back to their respective vehicles. In the background Ryan is mumbling as he's making notes on his clipboard less than a hundred feet behind the three men. Brian gets to his SUV, unlocks it and gets in. He looks down at the passenger seat and there is another cell phone. A red one. It doesn't belong to him. He looks out and behind him through all the windows and then he gets out of his vehicle and looks around some more. Opening the passenger-side door, he decides that he's not going to turn it on. He grabs a plastic bag out of the glove compartment and slides the cell into it using a pen.

Just then, a voice comes over the radio. "We have a house fire on Sherwood Drive."

He climbs into his vehicle and gets on the radio and confirms it. "I'm less than ten minutes away and I am on route."

One of the other officers in the parking lot gets the same message and they look at each other. They both speed out of the parking lot with sirens on and lights flashing. Brian calls in on the radio as he looks around in his vehicle to see if anything else has been tampered with.

"Is anybody going to be at the fire who can analyze a cell phone?" he asks.

A voice from dispatch says, "I don't know what you're talking about . . . phone? What?"

"I have an extra cell phone that just showed up in my vehicle and I need to have it looked at from a forensic point of view. Fast," he explains.

"Not a problem. Mitch will be there on site. He's just dropping off the Marshall body."

The two officers are on full alert. Brian pulls into the site and a rapidly growing crowd is already gathering outside on the street. A one thousand-square-foot bungalow is up in flames in a quiet residential setting. Brian gets out of his vehicle and walks over to the fire chief.

"How did it start? How long has it been going on? Better yet, what the fuck is going on in my town?" Brian inquires, momentarily losing his cool.

The chief replies, "This is a strange one because we got a random call ten minutes ago about a few puffs of smoke. When we got here, all hell broke loose— all the doors were zip-tied, and we're gonna have a hell of a time putting this out."

Brian looks back at the crowd and sees an exotic black De Tomaso Pantera car drive away from the scene.

He gets another call. "We have a distress call four miles north of town."

"What is it?" he asks.

Dispatch says, "Listen, Brian. This sounds like a strange one but some locals have complained that there are people in a pair of old outhouses under a tree."

"I don't have time for that. I have to stop by the courthouse and pick up those papers from the judge after this."

The dispatcher says, "You've got time, because the judge didn't show up . . . so if you want to go out there and figure that one out, I'll keep you posted on this end."

Brian calls Mitch over and shows him the red cell phone still in a bag sitting on the passenger side of his vehicle. The officer puts on some rubber gloves and uses a pen to turn it over. When he flips it over, he discovers it's covered in blood.

"What the hell is going on here?" Brian exclaims.

"Hey, I know who owns this cell phone," pipes up a third officer who is standing there. "That's the judge's phone."

Brian says, "Hold it. If this is the judge's phone, where is the judge? And whose blood is this?"

"Give me an hour," Mitch says. "I'll run over to the van and run it through the computer and see what we have."

Brian nods his head. The phone is bagged and taken across to a man a hundred feet away. Minutes later, the officer returns and says, "That was easy. It's Jeff Marshall's blood, and it is on our judge's phone."

Two hours goes by and Brian gets a call over the radio. "There's a lot going on, but it's clear now that there are two deceased bodies from this house fire. The bodies have been identified. They belong to the homeowners, Lynn and Gary Tobin." The fire marshal continues, "This was no accident. They were tied to seventy gallons of accelerant . . . each."

Brian walks through the crime scene. He takes his glasses off and puts them back on three or four times. He feels as if he must be missing something. A woman in a hoodie approaches and asks, "How did they die?"

He doesn't have time for this person, so he brushes her off with, "Probably smoke inhalation."

The woman states, "It looks like shish-kebab to me."

Brian turns around to talk to her and she's gone. Over his radio he hears, "Brian, come . . . Come see this. You've got to see this! This is straight out of a horror movie." "What now?"

"We're just outside of town at the outhouse call." The officer's voice trembles. "You've got to come and see this! I'm going to rope this thing off and quarantine it and I'm calling the feds."

"Christ, can't we do this without having brass up our ass?" Brian asks. He races out of the parking lot, screeches down the suburban street and heads to Erskine Park, just outside of town.

When he pulls up, there are six cruisers with their lights flashing. He gets out and says, "What in the hell is going on here?"

They lift up the tape and let him walk under it and he walks through some tall grass and then he gets to the first outhouse. He looks around and there are half a dozen big trees. A porta potty is located directly below them. He opens the door slowly . . . and there is the judge. He has been stripped naked and he is hanging by a rope that protrudes through the top of the outhouse and is fastened to the tree limb above it. He has random stickers all over his body, advertising everything from oil companies to baby shampoo brands. A blue bandana is tied around his eyes. His testicles have been slit open and are lying on the floor.

Brian steps back, covering his nose and mouth. "There's more?"

The officer says, "Eight males and two females: the judge, two female officers, three mercenaries and two D.A.s, Terry Bird and John Bell."

"Why in the hell is this happening in my jurisdiction? This is my town," Brian says in bewilderment.

The tall officer takes Brian aside. "Is it any coincidence that three of the deceased all had a beef with Odan at one time?"

Brian replies, "That's preposterous! He's been a pillar in our community for so long now."

"Okay, but explain this to me, Chief. Where did you just come from?"

"What a dumb-ass question . . . a house fire," Brian states.

"The people who died in that house were none other than Odan's ex-wife and her husband. Where were you this morning? Or do I have to remind you? You were at the scene where someone got stabbed and bleached . . . yet another someone who didn't much admire Odan, to be put lightly. Let's bring him in for questioning."

"No, not yet," Brian replies. "He hates us already. We have zero proof he had anything to do with any of this."

Back in the plane, Odan sounds off, "We need to take a swing west and keep that marker on our left side while we go down in the valley."

They make a steep bank and another pilot can be heard saying over the radio, "We have a pipeline laid up there. We're going to go on signal and fly it."

Odan says, "Can we get this thing at twenty-two hundred feet, so we can get a little bit of a map going on?"

"Roger," the pilot replies.

"Hold it steady on the DCF specs and we'll shoot the map over the next four miles," the co-pilot replies.

They finish the program and sign off and Odan says to the pilots, "Let's give this little girl a flyby over her home."

"Copy that," a voice comes from the cockpit.

"Let's grab her down, boys. Let's even try an eight-fifty," Odan says.

"But Odan, we'll get in shit for that."

"Don't worry, boys, I'll just tell him that I'm spraying virgin cherries before they pop," he explains.

The pilots in the front chuckle. "Hey boys, what can we stall at?" the co-pilot asks.

"Odan, are you sure you want to try that?" the pilot says.

"What? Crashing a plane and going down in history is popping cherries! Besides, you guys know how to fly," Odan states.

The speed is cut back just barely over stall, as they fly over Trace's house. Her dad is out on the porch. He looks up, disturbed.

She opens the bubble window in the plane and can see he's agitated with the low flying plane and she yells, "Sorry, Dad!"

"He can't hear you over the engine," Odan says, smiling. Just then Trace gets a text message from her brother.

Where the hell are you?

In an airplane doing a fire scout, she replies.

With him? he asks.

Yes, we've been up for a few hours. Don't worry. We'll be on the ground soon. We're ten from the final approach.

Have you heard about all the shit that's going on down here?

Sarcastically, she replies, *One less drug dealer.*

A dozen murders in the last forty-eight hours. All of the vics despised your boy toy, he texts.

What? Wow! And…why do you keep saying "boy toy"? Because he's not, and it doesn't make any sense. He's a good guy and I've been with him the whole time. We're landing soon. I'll have to talk to you a little later, she types and she ends the text.

They circle around, tilting the plane to the left at a thirty-degree angle. Trace is now looking down at her own home from under nine hundred feet.

"Get your cell out and take a picture. This is a good time because we're not coming back," Odan says.

She pulls out her cell phone and sticks it at the bubble window and takes nine pictures of the home and the area. The plane levels out, and she can hear the pilot say, "Glass nose, requesting to land on two-seven."

He executes a near-perfect landing with a little shaking going on from the left wheel of the tricycle-geared airplane. She texts Brian:

We just landed and we're pulling up to the hangar.

Odan and Trace leave the airplane while it is still running and head over toward the parking lot. Pulling up to the hangar at the same time is Jon, driving his father's old Jaguar. Trace looks over to Odan and says, "Your son is pulling up to the hangar."

He replies, "Yeah, he took the old Jag in to get some strut work done."

Odan gently puts his right hand on the small of her back. He says, "How was that?"

"I think I should be the one asking you that question. How did you like the view, Odan? And I'm not talking about the view out the window," she says, smiling.

"I—I—I . . . it wasn't intentional. I didn't know you would be wearing a short skirt today. Besides which part are you talking about? Me being observant, or you watching me catch a glimpse of your panties?" he says with a wink.

"So, what are you doing for dinner tonight?" she asks with a school-girl smile, biting the corner of her lip.

"I was planning to just stay home and barbecue and have a few vegetables," he states.

"So . . . what time do you want me there?" she asks coyly.

He grins. "Ah, it doesn't matter. I should be home by four-thirty so any time after that," he says, trying to hide his pleasure at her coming over.

"How about I bring over some fruit and we can make smoothies?" she suggests. "Deal," he replies. He helps her into her car and gives her a kiss on her cheek. As he's closing her door, Kelly comes walking out of the hangar.

"Are you going to tap that?" he says.

Shaking his head in disbelief, Odan waves as Trace drives away. "Kelly, Kelly, Kelly," he says, then jumps into his black truck. He pulls up next to him and rolls his window down.

"Can't you see it? She wants you to make the next move," Kelly replies.

"I think I've gone as far as I'm going to go with her," Odan says.

Kelly replies quickly, "Fuck that noise. Where is the old Odan? Do you know the one? The guy who could go into any room and do whatever he wanted with whoever he wanted, because that's just who he was . . . I want that guy back. You know, the guy who didn't take shit from anybody. You remember what Teyo used to call you?" He pauses for a moment. "He used to call you OG."

"That guy is gone," Odan says.

"And she's taken the other guys' balls with him," says Kelly.

Odan's cell phone rings and he sees that it's Trace. He walks away from Kelly to take the call in private.

"Miss me already?" he growls.

"Odan, I hope I'm not out of line here, but I have to know what happened to the journal that was in your office," she says.

He stops dead in his tracks. "I honestly thought you took it or moved it," he says.

"No—why would I do that?" she says. "It's just . . . it was the only thing I could see that was missing in the house. And then, of course, there was whatever made you come running out of your bedroom like the place was on fire."

"Some keys to some very private things," he says. He has a pensive look on his face and he says, "I'll see you tonight. I have to go." Then he ends the call.

Trace turns on the stereo and then off again. Her cell phone lights up and she thinks it's Odan calling her back, but it's Brian. A picture of his face is displayed as the caller but he is fifteen years old in the picture. "Where are you?" he asks.

"Where do you think I am? I'm driving home," she replies.

"There have been fourteen homicides in my district in the last forty-eight hours," he tells her.

"I fail to see what that has to do with me," she replies.

"I'm not doing stories on gang-related problems in your kitchen," Brian states. "Let me put it to you simply. You're doing a story on a guy, and a bunch of people who have had grievances with him are showing up dead. I've got a bunch of suits running around, telling me they're looking for a suspicious character in relation to the crimes, but as fucking funny as it may sound to some, they won't give me a description. I've also had a lot of reports of a white Ford half ton in the vicinity of these crime scenes."

"And . . .?" she replies.

"Doesn't he own a fleet of white Ford half tons?" Brian asks.

"Give your head a shake, Brian. Maybe I'm gonna buy myself a white Ford half ton and trade in my Mercedes. That's it, that's what I gotta do. I'll get the best deal. I'm done with your shit. This is totally ludicrous."

"Where did all this vulgar language come from?" he asks.

She smiles and rolls down the window on the passenger side, steps on the gas and says, "One week here. I thought I was going to have a quiet, relaxing time and look at what has happened."

"Yeah, let's reflect on that for a second," he says. "You got drunk. You're hanging around with shady people."

"Yeah, I'm hanging around with you," she states.

She hangs up and calls home. Her mom answers. She pushes for an explanation, "Mom, what has happened to this place? It's full of crooked judges, crooked cops, and I don't know what to think anymore."

Her mom paces the floor and replies, "Times . . . people change. Sometimes it brings the best out of folks and sometimes not. But when it comes to Odan, I'm going to give you a heads-up for your article. He's a good guy . . . one of the few. He took on that little boy when he didn't have to and everybody thought he had some ulterior motive, but years later, we now know he did it for the right reasons. He's a dreamer, that's for sure. But still, be careful, because he has . . . how do I say it? A colourful side that not everyone appreciates."

"So what does Brian have so against him, then?" Trace asks.

"Well, let me put it this way," her mom explains. "Brian had a girlfriend and she was a good one, but because of advice she got from Odan, she followed her career and left."

"Crap! Why didn't someone tell me this a long time ago?" Trace asks.

"I'm sorry, Trace. Your brother's sensitive about it, and apparently he didn't think you needed to know," her mom says.

Downtown. Two-thirty p.m. At the local bistro, Bass and his partner, Dag, are dressed in business attire without ties. Bass is drinking a green juice and his partner is drinking a coffee. Dag appears to be ten years older and less concerned about his health. Bass says, "She's here. How are you going to handle this?"

Just then Dag's cell phone rings and it is Janice Breaker. "How close are you to turning this off?" she asks.

Bass looks across the table and says, "Forty-eight hours, tops."

In a controlled tone, Janice says, "We don't have forty-eight hours. The word on the wire is, if she's coming to kick down the door, it's in our house. Let's just say, we don't have the time and we don't have the luxury of waiting any longer. Tap into any of the local enforcement. Do whatever you have to do. But tie this off now."

A woman sits down with them. Bass says to her, "Can I help you? This is a private conversation."

The woman says, "I can help you. In fact, I can help you find her tonight. I'm going to a barbecue."

Dag covers up the receiver on the cell phone with a red cloth napkin. "And who the hell are you?" he asks.

"I live here. I was a reporter at one point in time. Now I do a little bit of investigating for some local friends. My brother was killed and his hands were removed. I think you know what I'm talking about," she says.

The street lights come on, reflecting on their faces. Dag grabs the cell and says, "Janice, I gotta call you back," and he hangs up.

Mason. Two forty-five p.m. A blond, busty lady answers the door of her home and receives a package. She turns and walks into her kitchen. She picks up her phone and calls her husband.

"Honey, you're not gonna believe this. We just got a restaurant gift card and a pair of plane tickets dropped off at our house," she says. "It doesn't say who they're from."

Peter Derickson says to his wife, "That's cool," in a nonchalant tone.

"Can I check into it?" she asks.

"Why not? Are there dates on it?" he asks.

"Yes," she replies. "The gift card has to be used tonight, and the flight has to be used within forty-eight hours."

"What the hell? Let's do it, if it's real. You check it out before I get home. I'll be home by five."

The lady hangs up the phone and starts calling to verify the gifts, as she rolls herself a joint. After placing a couple of calls, she calls her husband back and says, "We're on for The Lizard and Chicken at five-thirty tonight. Don't be late."

"Not a problem, I'll be home in time," he replies and hangs up. He looks up at the prostitute in the motel room and exclaims, "Fuck, this is sore! I was playing cards last night. I lost a bet and the bet was this stupid, ass-fucking tattoo. Got drunk and I didn't care. I don't understand why it says 'Don't resuscitate.' All I won all night was a goddamn pencil."

Peter slips on his shirt and pants and looks down at the checkout slip for room twenty-eight of the Racoon Motel. He puts his watch back on that also has a medical alert on it.

Meanwhile, his wife is at home on the phone booking a flight for her and her husband to go to Vegas the next morning at eleven a.m.

Brian takes a call in his office. He answers it, "Brian Scott."

The polite voice on the other end says, "My name is Lisa Jackson. I'm here in your city with Catarina Wanderbelt. We are broker bankers. I'm from Atlanta and my associate is from the Netherlands. We need to speak with you in person, as soon as possible."

"Can someone else talk to you? I'm really busy. We've had a big round of trouble as of late," Brian asks.

"No, it has to be you and only you. This has to do with the trouble you've been having lately. We're staying at the Raccoon Motel. We can meet you later in the day if that works for you."

He ponders for a moment, looks out the window and says, "I may be able to meet you for a brief bite to eat at about six."

"That'll be fine. Where would you like to meet?" she asks.

He says, "There's a place called The Lizard and Chicken."

"We'll find it," she says, and she hangs up the phone.

Trace gets a call as she's in the kitchen with her mother, drinking a cup of coffee. She answers her phone, "Hello."

"Hello, young lady. This is Gary, you know the Gary who is going to get an article from you shortly," he says.

"I'm working on it," she says.

He asks, "Would you like to join me for supper? Apparently, I've won an extravagant gift certificate for The Lizard and Chicken and I have to use it tonight."

"I have plans tonight, so I wish I could make it, but I can't," she says.

"If you don't mind me asking, what are these big plans that you have that you can't enjoy a nice dinner on the house?" he asks.

There's a delay as she drinks a mouthful of coffee and puts it down on the island. "Well, it's kind of complicated, but I've been invited to a barbecue at Odan's."

She is treated to dead silence for twenty seconds and then she asks, "Are you still there?"

"Did you say you're going to his house?" he asks.

She pauses as she gazes up at her mom, "Yeah, it's complicated. It'll be the second time I've been out there."

Gary stands up and goes to his office window. "Is there a story there?"

"Maybe . . . Are you worried?" she asks.

"About what?" he says. "Something that happened a long time ago? Not a bit. He's not that kind of a guy. We all screwed him . . . not proud of it, but it happened. It's done with now."

She finishes her coffee and puts it in the sink. "Did you know there are people turning up dead who have messed with him in the past? Have you heard of karma? Good night, Gary. Oh, and enjoy!" she says, and she pushes the End button on her cell.

Odan calls from a low-slung red sports car going very fast through the valley. "Kelly, what are you up to?"

Kelly replies, "I've been ordered to kill some time today."

"Can I ask you a question?" Odan asks.

"Sure, fire away," he replies.

"The cabin is twenty-eight feet tall and I can get a permit to put it up to thirty-four feet to avoid a little crawlspace where the furnace is. How much work is involved and can you do it?" Odan asks.

"Anything is possible but you gotta remember to stay above the water table." "Oh, I forgot to ask you . . . Can you come to my place for a barbecue tonight? Ryker and I are having some family and friends over," Odan states.

"What time is the barbecue? I want to bring over some blueprints for that stone-and-glass shack you want to build on 50 Ave. Do you think it's all right, with all the craziness out there?" Kelly asks, not sure if Odan knows what's happening, because he knows Odan doesn't listen to the radio.

"Six works, bring the side elevations and a box of pencils. I've got the floor plans with me," Odan states.

"Then I'm hurrying, because I got some time to kill," says Kelly, chuckling.

10

Chase

Ryan gets a call in his office.

"Ryan, this is Robert," he states. "It seems we've got a suspicious lady poking her nose around at our site."

"That's just great! We've got three open houses today and the grand opening of our new design," Ryan replies. "Do you think we should call the big guy?"

"No way. Let's handle it ourselves," Robert states.

"Can you meet me out there at four-thirty?" asks Ryan.

Robert replies back, "Don't forget we have the barbecue tonight at six." "Damn, I almost forgot," says Ryan.

"Shouldn't be a problem. It's probably nothing anyways, and you know how the big guy is. He won't be happy if we don't check it out."

"Okay. By the way, did you hear about the new girl?" Ryan replies. "Well, I guess she's not new, exactly," he adds. "She used to live here years ago and she's the police chief's sister."

"Is she? Oh wow, I didn't know that," says Robert.

"Yeah, she's supposed to be some big-time reporter who has come back here after her divorce."

Robert says, "The big guy doesn't stand a chance, does he?"

East side of the lake. Butterflies flutter above a six-foot-six slender man walking along an abandoned walkway. He's got long grey hair and wears a silver silk suit. He has a water bottle half full of tequila and a week-old beard. Suddenly, a twenty-inch arrow hits him in the side of the thigh, and before he falls to the ground, four more hit him, two in the front and two from the left side.

From the trees a man and woman, one hundred yards apart, scurry away. The tall man's hand does not let go of the bottle. It remains in his hand.

Brian comes out of the change room at the station and everybody is in a sombre mood. There is no chatter. A lady approaches him with some papers and asks, "What are our plans for Donna's funeral?"

He replies, "Take it up with HR. Her family will take care of it." He goes into his office and puts his head in his hands at his desk. Then there's a knock on his door. Two men walk through it and the younger one asks to close the door. They pull out their identification and leave it on his desk for a moment.

Brian leans over the desk and asks, "So what can I do for the feds today?"

Bass leans back and crosses his legs while adjusting his suit. The other officer sits forward and places his elbows on the arms of the chair. He states, "It seems we've made a mistake."

Brian stands up and asks, "What kind of mistake? Because your timing is absolutely the shits."

"We believe that someone bad has found their way here," the older gentleman says.

Brian replies, "No . . . you don't say? The funeral business is booming here and that's ironic, because we have a large population of seniors. I'm keeping all these deaths from everybody—not even their families know what's going on. I can only hold off till tomorrow. The only one that squeaked by me was Jeff Marshall. Shit, there's a barbecue going on tonight for a family and they don't even know one of their parents was killed."

"Can you keep us posted of anything strange?" the older one asks.

Brian walks over to his door and opens it. "Go fuck yourself. Get out . . . I can find you if I need you!"

Bass walks to the door and Brian walks up beside Dag, who's still sitting. A foot away from Dag, Brian takes the leather restraint off his sidearm and stares at the floor, with an annoyed look on his face. The two men leave. Brian adjusts himself and goes and sits behind his desk. He looks up at a football picture of him and Odan. It is the picture he took from Odan's house the other night. Odan's arm is around his shoulder and a trophy is at their feet. He looks down and flips over the paper that Trace had given him and there is a list of profiles of the individuals she has researched.

Deep in the valley, on a twisty, windy road overlooking the lake, Odan is pulled over for speeding in his red Rimac.

The tall officer who pulls him over says to him, "Ninety-one is way too fast for here. What's your hurry?"

Odan shakes his head, pulling his hands down from the steering wheel and says, "Why does it matter how fast I'm driving way out here? There's not another car on the road. If I hit a raccoon or a deer, it'll be my own fault," he says.

"Why do you have to piss in my cornflakes? I'm just trying to do my job," the policeman replies.

Click. Odan opens his door and the officer backs up. The officer notices his eyes are wet. Odan reaches his right hand out to shake hands with the officer. The officer responds in the same way.

"Thank you, and I'm sorry," Odan mumbles.

"I'm not going to rip this ticket up. You still have to pay it," the officer says in a polite, professional voice.

"I know," Odan says. "And I heard about your loss. I was going too fast back there. I'm sorry for giving you a hard time on a day like today. I wasn't paying attention. I was just blowing off a little steam and I thought up here would be the perfect place to do it."

The officer replies, "It's not a problem, but just take note—this is my patrol day and time to patrol this road, in case you ever want to blow off steam again."

Odan smiles at the police officer and goes back to his Taurus cruiser. Odan's red sports car pulls away from the shoulder without a sound and reaches the speed limit in under three seconds.

Back in Mason at the police headquarters, Brian steps out of the office and asks an officer sitting at a worn desk, "Could you drive me home?"

The officer replies, "Sure, Chief. But why do you need a ride home?"

"I just wanna leave my car here tonight and relax," responds Brian, trying to avoid telling the officer he does not want his vehicle out tonight. In his mind he feels he's being followed.

The officer says, "Sure, my cruiser is parked in the garage."

"Perfect!" Brian says. "Are you going soon, because anytime works for me."

The officer says, "Give me a minute to book out."

With a sigh and a nod of approval, Brian acknowledges the officer. The two of them walk down toward the garage. At the bottom of the concrete stairs, Brian stops at a desk. He asks the plain-clothed man sitting there, "Can I see the judge's cell phone?" The officer brings him the bloody cell phone in a bag, and he puts it on the metal counter. Brian picks it up with his left hand and turns it over. Holding the cell in his right hand, he asks without looking up at the other man, "Have they run this thing for evidence?"

Shrugging his shoulders, the man behind the desk says, "Yeah, it's all done . . . you're good to go. They finished with it about an hour ago. They're just waiting until Monday to get a court order to activate it—at least that's what they told me upstairs."

"I'm signing it out. I'll have it back here before Monday," Brian says as he leans over and picks up the pen that is lying on the counter. Avoiding making any eye contact, Brian signs it out. Discarding the pen after it rolls off the counter, Brian takes the cell and he and the officer continue through a set of doors. They get into the cruiser and shut their doors in unison. The electric garage door opens in front of them and the officer puts the car into Drive. They drive out of the building as the man with the rune stone thumb ring sits and watches them from a car parked across from the police station. Then he pulls away from the curb in an unassuming grey Nissan sedan.

At four p.m., Odan walks into the greenhouse and says, "How are you doing, darling?" He's greeted with a big hug from Gwen. She gives him a little shake and after a second they stand back and he says, "Don't forget the barbecue tonight."

"You bet ya. Is there anything you want me to bring? Gwen asks.

Odan responds in a playful tone, "No. Just Al, and make sure you're on time . . . See if he can accidentally leave his cigarettes at home, please and thank you, if you know what I mean. Oh, and say hi to Chuckles and Dawn for me."

As Odan walks away, Gwen calls out, "Who else is going to be there?"

"My family, you guys and a couple of friends."

She giggles and says, "Your family is going to be there? Are you sure you shouldn't rent a hall?"

"Too funny, Firestone . . . see ya there."

On his way back into town, Odan sees a house for sale and he watches a blue Jag pull up in front of it. The car has a female realtor's picture on the side and her name, Jaclyn Ball. A young, curvaceous woman gets out and walks into the house. Odan decides to pull in. He parks his car behind hers in the driveway. With confidence, he walks up to the door and rings the doorbell.

The Botoxed, tanned, blond woman is wearing a short summer dress and answers the door barefoot. "Hello, can I help you?" she asks.

He walks through the door. He looks at her bare feet and notices she has an unusual gap between her big and second toes. Casually, he asks, "Would you mind showing me this house? I was just driving by . . ."

She doesn't recognize him. She replies, "Absolutely! But I've only got twenty minutes before my next showing."

He walks past her and looks around then comments, "Nice open concept and clean look." He continues, "This is your listing, correct?"

"Uh-huh!" she says, gazing over her shoulder at herself in a full-length mirror at the base of the stairs.

"How long has it been on the market?" Odan questions.

"I listed it about a year ago," the realtor replies.

"Is the roof a four-twelve pitch?" he asks.

"I don't know," she says apologetically.

"What kind of wood are these railings?" Odan asks.

"I'm not sure," she says with a smile.

He walks into the living room and touches the window and asks, "Is this R-20 insulation?"

"I'm sure it is," she replies.

"Are these windows argon-filled?"

"The windows are expensive. They're high-end," she replies, puckering her lips, and adjusting her hair.

He takes a second and rubs his chin. "You know the biggest thing that pisses me off?"

"What?" Jaclyn asks, smiling.

He stares at her with an intense look and says, "It's putting lipstick on a pig—or should I say, when you get a female realtor who hasn't got the first damn clue what she's selling and a poor bastard like me comes by and sinks a million into it, and pays you a commission for doing absolutely nothing but sticking your tits out." He continues, "If you were working for me, I would've skidded your ass. You would starve without that thing between your legs."

He turns and walks out the door, shaking his head in disbelief and disappointment. The realtor's jaw is frozen like an ice cube in the tray in the freezer.

Odan's phone rings as he approaches his car but he doesn't answer it until he's inside and the doors are closed. His rear tires give off a school-girl screech as he leaves the curb.

"Dyno? Dyno, when are you coming to get me?" the little voice says.

"Ryker, Dyno will be there to get you in twenty minutes," Odan says.

"Okay, Dyno. I've got my shoes on and I'm ready to go."

"Are they on the right feet?" asks Odan, playfully.

"Yip, yip," Ryker says.

"See you soon," Odan assures him, as he hangs up.

Before he goes to pick up Ryker, he stops by his waste management business. As he pulls up into the three-acre parking lot in front of the pole shed, Odan notices that there are two company trucks there already. One of the trucks belongs to Robert and one of the trucks belongs to Ryan. On the right-hand side is an office, which consists of a tan fourteen-hundred-square-foot stucco home and a variety of landscaping equipment. The immaculate one-hundred-foot-long metal pole shed sits in front of the yard and is used to store sea cans, dump bins, porta potties and zoom booms.

Odan walks toward the office and both Ryan and Robert are just leaving. The three men meet three quarters of the way into the yard and shake hands.

Odan asks, "What brings you guys out here?"

Robert pauses, looks at Ryan and says, "We had a report of a suspicious person out here and we just came to check if anything has been tampered with before we go to the barbecue."

"And, what did you find?" asks Odan.

Ryan replies, "We can't find a damn thing. Just small footprints with a long stride. It was a female, I think. She was here poking around in the back of the building and she left. We have a glimpse of her on camera coming out the back. We have no idea how she got in and it doesn't look like she took anything. She moves like a shadow . . . almost like a ghost."

Robert adds, "We can't get a description of her other than she appears to be a little older but in great shape. Her stride is like an athlete's."

"How can you be sure it's a female? I take it you guys did a walk-through?" asks Odan.

Ryan replies, "Yes, we did, and we can't find anything out of place. Considering everything in here is big . . . there's no small pumps or tools she could have taken. Everything that's small is locked up in the pole shed, and that wasn't touched. Answering your question about how we know it's a female, when you check out the video for yourself you can tell. She's got some pretty sharp edges, excluding the headlights and caboose . . . I've sent the video to your romance email sight, you can look at it for yourself."

The three men start walking toward their vehicles and Ryan looks over his shoulder, cocks his head and continues, "There might have been a couple of things that were by the front of the pole shed yesterday that I didn't see today—a shovel and some rope."

Robert replies, "I haven't been here for a week, so I wouldn't know."

"I don't have time to dick with this, so just leave it for now," Odan says. "I'll see you at the barbecue in a little over an hour . . . and, by the way, how the hell do you know about my romance site?"

"I've known for some time that you're writing these so-called romantic books and you're trying to keep it secret, Boss," Ryan says. "*Playing with a Broken Moon* was left open on your iPad one day. Whatever you do, don't let my wife see that shit—she's already distracted enough with the kids."

Ryan and Robert are doing everything in their power not to smile. Simultaneously, all three get into their vehicles and drive away.

Odan gets a call as he's climbing into his car.

"Hi, Trace here. I hate to bother you, but I think I'm going to have to take a rain cheque on the barbecue tonight if that's okay?"

"That's not okay. I expect you there and that's all there is to it," he replies brusquely. As he drives off the site, his tone turns more playful. "Furthermore, I didn't invite any cops this time . . . and you get an opportunity to meet my family and friends in a social setting—isn't that what you've been wanting?"

"Okay, I'll come," she says, "on one condition."

"What's that?" Odan asks.

"Is it okay if I come dressed super casual?" she says.

Odan smiles and replies. "I'll feed my family Ritalin before you get there, and . . . I'll give you money for an Uber?"

Smiling back, Trace states, "You're an ass, but yeah, I'll be there . . . but I can't guarantee Brian won't crash it."

"I couldn't help notice your bellybutton ring in the airplane today," he blurts out without thinking.

"Yeah, and I couldn't help notice you noticing my bellybutton ring and my ankle bracelet today. That's good. Every girl likes a man who pays attention to detail," Trace says.

"I promise, if you make it through this, I will take you somewhere special tomorrow," he says.

She says with a chuckle in her voice while biting her lip, "I know you're driving right now, but if you weren't driving, I'd be picturing you with your hands in your front pockets."

Playfully, Odan replies, "Oh yeah? Well, right now I'm envisioning you biting your lip. I'll see you there. Don't be late," he repeats, knowing she feels his smile. He presses End on his cell.

Knowing he has to pick up Ryker shortly, Odan pulls into the hangar and drives the car inside, turns it off, and notices a light in his office up on the mezzanine. He walks up into his office to find two men standing in his office, not touching anything but looking around. "Can I help you?" he asks.

"I'm agent Dag from CIT, and I'm looking for some information," the man in the suit says in a clipped tone.

"CIT . . . what's that stand for? Cocksuckers in transit?" Odan asks in a sarcastic voice. There is a huge delay as he smiles at the men, staring at them coldly. Then he continues, "Listen, fellas . . . you transgender, government wannabes, I'm in the aviation industry, I have a restaurant, and I'm trying to build a winery. I deal with government people all day long, so cut the shit. Why are you here?" he asks.

Agent Bass states, "We're looking for a lost person."

"Let me help you guys out. In fact, out of my office, because apparently you guys are lost yourself. Go, go," he asserts as his voice rises. When they don't immediately move, Odan grabs the agents by their triceps and squeezes, as he moves the men toward the opening in the hangar. He shuffles them out his door like small school children. "Don't come back until you've washed your hands," he says, never breaking a stride, only a smile.

As the two agents walk back to their vehicle, Bass turns and says, "It's you that was lost and now we found you."

Odan replies looking at Bass, "Batman, take the Riddler and get the fuck out of my site!"

"We'll be back," says Dag, as they get in their tan Tahoe and roll down the windows.

"So will gonorrhoea if I bang your mother without a toque," Odan retorts. Attempting to stare him down from the passenger seat, Bass says, "Listen, asshole, we said we'll be back."

"You listen here, thunder thighs . . . I'll save you a trip. I already have a butt plug." The men drive away, squealing their tires. Odan stares after them as they drive all the way off the lot. He then goes to the side of the hangar, turns all the lights off and gets back in his truck. The scissor doors close. The sound of his Coyote V8 echoes off the concrete and the trees as he comes back down into the valley from the airport. He pulls up in front of a home that's situated in a quiet close, halfway between his work and his home. Odan goes up to the door, leaving his driver's door open. The little blond boy, Ryker, is there to greet him and he grabs his hand.

As they walk back to the truck, Ryker is staring up at him. "Dyno . . . is Grampa going to be there?"

Odan replies, bending down to the boy's level, in a soft, clear voice, "I hope so. He's getting better." He then releases the boy's hand and places his fingertips on the little boy's back, nudging him ahead and saying, "Hurry up, jump in and buckle yourself up."

Ryker runs up to the open door, scampers in and quickly buckles himself in as Odan approaches the truck, smiling. Bubba stands watching from the window with a smile on her face. Reminiscing, she uncrosses her arms and puts her hands in her front pockets. She then brings her hands toward each other until they almost touch. She holds her breath. As Odan drives, she closes her eyes, lets out her breath and gathers herself. One hand in her pocket, she walks down the hallway quickly to her bedroom and closes the door behind her.

Odan turns on the radio and a Gin Blossoms song is playing. "What's that?" Ryker asks.

"What's what?" Odan says, turning his head and locking eyes with the blue-eyed boy. Ryker reaches over and turns the volume down as he rolls down his window.

The little boy points out the window with his finger. "That." The faint echo of multiple sirens and squealing tires are heard off in the distance, as Odan rolls down his window.

"Nothing to worry about. It has nothing to do with us . . . we'll read all about it on Facebook in an hour," Odan states gently and calmly as he places his right hand on the little boy's shoulder. He rolls the windows back up and drives the balance of the three miles to their place. A half dozen vehicles, including three white Ford trucks, are parked in his driveway.

Meanwhile, the police are on the lookout for a speeding car that has been spotted in both Coldstream and the Mission area in Mason. An officer says on the radio, "It looks like an older car, but is it ever aerodynamic. What kind of car is that?"

Another officer's voice chimes in, "Guys, it's a Pantera. A DeTomaso, to be exact. It's been seriously modified. It's been playing with us—I tried to stop it up on Rabbit Hill. It was seen along with a white Ford half ton at one of the crime scenes earlier. The cameras also caught a silver Corvette."

A voice asks, "Doesn't Odan own a silver 'Vette?"

Another voice comes over the radio, "He was driving that red Rimac today because I gave him a ticket."

"He's usually driving that black pickup," someone else says.

Just then, a bulletin comes over the radio, "We have a report of a female homicide victim at the Raccoon Motel."

A female officer replies, "Should we call Brian?"

Another voice states softly, "Just leave him alone. He's got a bit of time off, let him enjoy it. I'll tell him when he comes in tomorrow afternoon."

Two officers go to the Raccoon Motel to investigate. One of them asks questions while the other looks through the crime scene. A short Black woman in her forties has been found dead in her bathtub of apparent drowning. Wearing a pair of gloves and using a four-inch metal pointer, the officer gently opens the wallet on the dresser to find her identification. The coroner is on site with the investigation team.

The officer states on the radio, "It appears the victim is Lisa Jackson, a banker from Atlanta."

Just then, a detective walks past him into the bathroom. He can be heard saying out loud, "It's wine . . . somebody drowned her in white wine."

Suddenly an officer is heard yelling outside, "Stop! Stop! Stop or I'll shoot!" Shots ring out in the parking lot, and the smell of metal and fired guns rises in the air as a black-and-grey Pantera drifts out of the lot to the left, sliding perfectly between the oncoming traffic and speeding down the road, just narrowly missing a family with an infant in a stroller crossing the street.

Three officers gather in the parking lot. One says, "Did you get a description?" Another one replies, "It was a female."

"We've got to find that car!" one officer shouts.

"You got a shot off. What did you hit?" asks the youngest officer.

A small Asian man sitting on the sidewalk says, "He got her in the arm."

The officers hurry over to question the man. Before they get directly in front of him, the man continues, "I didn't see anything, just a fast woman jumping in a fast car and that fat cop over there shot her in the arm. She's fast. She must be some kind of gymnast."

"How tall is she?" one of the officers asks.

"It happened so fast." The bystander adds, "Maybe she's five foot seven, maybe . . . athletic build. She's very attractive."

"I get the picture, old man . . . a hot chick," the fat officer states.

The Asian man stands and glares up at the officer. "Listen, you fat bastardized Crisco eatin' cab driver. My name is Frank Lu. I'm eighty. I said woman, not chick. I hope she finds you in an alley and kicks the cellulite out of you."

Four blocks away from the crime scene, Gary Adelle is now driving thirty miles per hour along Lakeshore Drive. He's coming up on a red light at Contemporary Avenue in his red Jaguar ragtop, with a bald man in a Chevy Malibu in front of him, when he hears a car coming up behind him rapidly. The dark two-tone grey Pantera is rapidly closing in on his rear bumper. He tries to stop, gripping the steering wheel with both hands. He feels his brakes fading and pushes the pedal all the way to the floor, but little happens. He veers his car to the right and it jumps the curb and he runs it into some four-foot-tall caragana bushes. The Pantera races through the red light, followed by a silver Corvette.

Thinking it's perhaps teenagers, Gary Adelle calls his wife and says, "I need the brakes worked on the car. We're going to have to take your car to dinner. I'll call a tow truck and the dealer. Can pick me up at the corner of Lakeshore and Contemporary?"

"Sure, hon," his wife replies and ends the call.

Three police cars cruise by with their sirens off but their lights on. Minutes pass by and a tow truck and Gary's wife soon appear. Gary hands his key fob to the truck driver and gives him a quick nod. Then he jumps in his wife's Lexus SUV and they head off to The Lizard and Chicken.

Odan gets a call on the phone. "Mr. Harrison, this is Officer Herbert, James Herbert. May I ask you where you are right now?"

"I don't mean to be a dick, Officer Herbert, but I'm about three miles from home, not like it's any of your business," Odan says.

"Do you know where your Corvette is?" Herbert asks.

"No, I don't. Why do you ask?" Odan asks in an agitated tone.

"We've had some reports of reckless driving and suspicious behaviour by someone driving a silver Corvette like yours."

"It was at the hangar an hour and a half ago, I think. It's supposed to be parked there. It's not insured . . . Look, I have something else on my mind but as soon as I get to the house, I can take a look and see if the camera caught anything at the hangar. That sound good?" Odan replies.

"Yes, please and thank you, sir. I'll give you a call back in half an hour if that works for you?" states the officer.

"Sure, feel free to give me a call back," Odan replies.

Odan and Ryker pull up in front of his house. The little guy jumps out of the truck, grabs his backpack and runs to the house eagerly awaiting who he may see inside. Ryker opens the door but doesn't close it and Odan follows close behind him. The little blue-eyed boy drops his bag and runs downstairs where, he well knows, the rest of the kids will be.

Gwen comes out of the kitchen and gives Odan a big hug and says, "I've got some great news."

"Can you tell me on the way up to my office?" he asks.

They both walk through the house and up the spiral staircase to the turret, and Gwen says, "I got the papers! Thanks to you, I'm going to be spending a lot of time with my grandson in the future."

Odan turns to face her, "Good for you. I'm glad I could help." He logs on to the computer, standing up, and asks her, "Where's Al?"

"He's on the deck, chattin' it up with Robert and Ryan," Gwen explains.

Odan looks startled as he looks at his monitor and says, "Gwen, love, you're going to have to excuse me for a minute. I have to make a call."

"Not a problem," she replies, and she walks back down the metal stairs. Odan picks up his cell phone and dials the last number that came in. The whole time knowing something really sinister is in the works.

"Officer Herbert," the officer replies.

"My 'Vette is gone and our cameras only record when we shut things down. The cameras go on when the lights go off after a shift, so I don't know when it was taken ... it had to have been in broad daylight and we're on a fire watch right now, so everybody is busy. Find my car, please," Odan states humbly.

Officer Herbert asks, "Can you tell if there's anything else missing?"

"Oh my god! My 182 is missing!" Odan says.

"Sir, what is a 182?" asks the officer.

"A small plane, single engine, it's a Cessna. No, wait ... I'm looking on the video and someone is landing it right now," Odan replies, his voice rising.

"We'll send some cars out there immediately. Thanks."

"I'm clear across the other side of the city, an hour away," Odan says in an agitated tone. "Call me back. I'll text you the access code to the hangar and the video system so you can check it out."

"Thanks," the officer says, "we'll get back to you shortly. Stay put."

Three officers race to the hangar in two cruisers. When they get there they are greeted by two of Odan's employees. One of the men says to the officers, "Whoever they were are long gone. There was a man and woman who bailed out of the plane and drove away and where they went, I couldn't tell you."

An officer asks, "Can we just take a look around? Is it okay if we check inside the plane?"

"Absolutely. I'm the PRM—the person responsible for the maintenance of the plane," the man states. "You can look at the video, too, if you want."

One of the officers reviews the video and sees the two individuals. "They're both wearing gloves, and you're right, it looks like a man and a woman. Too blurry to make out any details other than that. They were fast, and they obviously knew what they were doing."

As the other officers approach the plane, they realize that the door on the right side of the plane has been removed and placed carefully on the ground. It appears as if something was moved out of the plane in a large bag. They all return to the office in the hangar after combing through the plane. After reviewing the video, the youngest officer puts the video on a jump drive to take with him for evidence. Everyone has thoughts they are not sharing. All the men, including the officers, leave the premises. The young officer is on his cell, texting Officer Herbert. Moments later, Odan misses a call from Herbert. The message left reads:

We have a jump drive and will give you a call in the morning. The hangar is locked up and we can't find the car but will be looking for it.

Meanwhile Brian is sitting at The Lizard and Chicken at the bar, waiting and having a cup of coffee. Lizzie walks up to him and taps him on the shoulder. "Are you sure you don't want a beer? It doesn't look like you're on duty," she asks with her girl-next-door smile.

"Yeah, sure. You can bring me a Coors or a Bud Light," Brian says.

"Since when did you start drinking light beer?" she asks.

"The whole damn department is on a brand-new fitness program and I barely passed stage one. I'm trying to set an example," he explains, as he rolls his eyes and tries to show her an unwilling right bicep.

"Why don't you go cop a squat in a comfortable booth over there and I'll bring you a beer," she suggests, tapping her fingernails on the bar. He grabs his coffee cup and walks across the restaurant and sits in the booth in the far corner facing the restaurant floor.

Lizzie comes by not a minute later with the beer. "Are you waiting for someone special?"

"Yeah, a couple of ladies from out of town are coming in twenty minutes. They want to talk to me," Brian says, attempting a professional tone.

"Ooooh, a couple of ladies . . . lucky guy," she says.

"It's not like that," he says. "It's job-related."

"What if their bitchin' hot virgin twins in their twenties . . . that all they need is a pair of handcuffs and some old-school discipline?" Lizzie teases, raising her eyebrows and giving him a playful nudge on the arm before she walks away.

Meanwhile, back at Odan's house at Kuusamo, smoke is filtering into the dining room from the barbecue. Odan realizes that he missed a call on his cell phone. He looks out the window and realizes Trace's car is out front. He walks into the living room and throws the bifold doors open onto the deck to find that Trace is having a conversation in a circle with his children, Leif, Stephanie and Danton.

Odan walks up to them and says good-naturedly, "Uh-oh. What kind of lies are you feeding her now?"

Stephanie replies, "Don't worry, Dad. We're just telling her the good stuff."

"Kids, if you don't mind, could I grab Trace for a moment, please?" Odan asks. "Of course," says Leif with an exaggeratedly accommodating lilt to his voice.

As they walk into the house and cross the floor toward the converted garage/rec room, Odan asks Trace, "Earlier today, did you see my Corvette in the hangar?"

"No, in fact, I thought I saw a guy get into it, in the driveway, when we were getting in the plane," Trace says.

"It's been stolen. Did you see what the guy looked like?" Odan asks.

"What? I assumed it was one of your guys. He was maybe a bit older," she replies.

"Shit, that means the car has been gone all day," he mumbles to himself, twisting his thumb ring around three hundred and sixty degrees.

Jon walks in the door with a dark-haired, eight-year-old boy in tan shorts and a blue T-shirt, and an attractive Asian woman in her early twenties. The woman is dressed in a gauzy white top, red shorts and stilettos.

Jon sees Trace and says, "Wow, you look great! Nice to see you again." As he approaches them, he turns to his father. "Hey, where are the dogs?"

Odan replies, "Tom is bringing them. He should be here shortly, but he had to deal with an issue at the airport."

Just then, Ryker runs in. "Dyno? Where are the puppies?" he asks.

Jon senses something off with his dad. Ryker and Jon's son, Julian, are positioned on either side of Odan, looking up at him. Jon steps forward, resting his palms on the boys' shoulders. Jon's eyes flit from the boys to his father.

"What's wrong, Dad?"

"Nothing." He sighs. "Everything," Odan says, as he turns and gently moves the boys and continues speaking with a gentle demeanour. "You guys go play, please and thank you."

"Everything?" Jon asks.

Looking through the window at the lake, Odan says wistfully, "I've had to rebuild my life so many times. You've never had to go through house arrest, humiliation, alienation for something you didn't do. You haven't been slammed by the news, wrongly convicted or had your dreams ripped from your heart out through your ass, but I have." Odan walks away, attempting to muster a smile for his guests. Trace is left standing in the middle of the room, uncertain of what just happened.

Back at The Lizard and Chicken, Brian waits. He's on his third beer. His cell indicates that the ladies are now officially late. He stares at a yellow school-issue pencil on the table that has suddenly appeared, as if by magic. He takes his fingers and rolls the pencil toward him and back again, feeling the flat sides as they make contact with the hard surface of the table.

Brian looks down at the folder sitting on the bench beside him and stares at it, scratching his chin with his index finger on his left hand. He brings the folder up and opens it. For a moment, he stares at the judge's cell phone, sitting inside in a plastic evidence bag. It is still covered in dried blood. Then, with some hesitation, he takes a cloth and the pencil and turns the phone on. The cell phone has been wiped and there are only two phone numbers on it. He dials the first number and it rings and rings. Brian takes a moment to gather himself. He hangs up and tries it again with the same response. On the third and final try, he listens to it ring twice and he hangs up. He sits back in his seat, staring at the phone, and goes to a quiet place in his mind to think.

The numbers on the phone are blocked, so Brian doesn't know who he's calling. He presses the dial button for the second number and it rings and someone answers. "The Scott residence." It's Brian's mother. He hangs up quickly. He puts the phone back in the bag and the folder and pushes it away in front of him and stares at it again. He ponders why a bloody phone belonging to the judge and with the blood of a drug dealer on it would have his parents' phone number on it.

He hears a familiar obnoxious voice as Peter Derickson and his wife come in and sit at a table in the middle of the restaurant. Right behind them are Gary Adelle and his wife, who are seated at a different table. Within five minutes, a number of contractors who used to work for Odan come through the restaurant. Kim Wilkes, a businessman who screwed Odan out of fifty grand years ago seats himself at the bar.

Brian gets up from the table and walks over to Gary. Gary looks up as he sees Brian approach.

"Don't you find it odd, Gary, that this restaurant is more or less full of people who don't like Odan?"

Gary looks around like a misguided owl. "Nah. I don't think anything of it. You have to remember, this is the best restaurant in the city, and just because things happened years ago doesn't mean anything now. If you want to know the truth, I'm here because I received a gift certificate for the restaurant that expires tomorrow, so maybe that's what these people are doing, too, cashing in on a free meal."

Brian gently knocks the knuckles of his right hand on the table and says, "You guys have a good night," and he walks back to his booth with a puzzled smile. More people who have betrayed Odan file in, confusing Brian. He sits back down on the bench, glancing between the patrons and the folder containing the cell, which has slipped and fallen on the floor, but the pencil has remained on the table.

Back at Kuusamo, Stephanie comes over and grabs Trace by her right elbow and walks her into the kitchen. A group of men are standing in a circle and Stephanie introduces Trace to them quickly.

"This is Walter, Khup, Tom, Fred, Gary, Book and . . . this is Eddie."

"Nice to meet you guys, I'll talk to you all shortly. I'm just going to make some rounds if that's okay?"

Gary states, "Of course. Not a problem."

The men move from the kitchen out to the deck. Jon and Leif are left making small talk over their second Naked Viking cocktail in the kitchen, while their girlfriends and Danton's date are out on the deck talking with Ryan, Al, Gwen, Robert and Odan's lawyer, Gregg.

More guests arrive. The sound of small children laughing and playing on the lower deck and out in the yard echoes above. Stephanie looks in the fridge and spies three trays of chocolates in ice cube trays and says to

Trace, "These are great. They're homemade. We have to try some—there are cherries inside. Dad makes these on special occasions."

A short man walks up to them and introduces himself, "I'm Dana. Listen, if you ever wanna marry and divorce Odan in the same year, call me." He smiles and chuckles as he shakes her hand and walks away.

"Nice to meet you . . . I think," she replies as he strolls away with a drink in hand. "Yeah, I bet these are awesome . . . the chocolates, I mean," Trace says, turning her attention back to Stephanie.

Jon starts chuckling and the chuckling quickly turns into a full-blown laugh. Trace and Stephanie walk over toward Leif and Jon and offer them chocolate.

Jon says, pointing to Leif, "Does he look like he needs more chocolate?"

The boys laugh and the girls walk away into the living room area. Trace puts a chocolate in her mouth and grabs another one as she sees Odan walk into his bedroom. She stands still for a couple of minutes as she eats the chocolates. The boys in the kitchen are laughing so loud that Leif's bellowing laugh can be heard throughout the house. Al's laugh is then heard all through the house from the deck.

Tom, dressed in a windbreaker and jeans, arrives at the house and opens the door with two puppies in tow; a brindle Great Dane and a red duck-tolling retriever run straight up to Trace and sit in front of her politely. Impressed, she reaches her hand out to them. They lick her hand and walk toward the bedroom.

She looks up. "They're amazing! Look at how well they're trained," she says to Tom. She can still hear the laughter spilling from the kitchen and the deck.

Jon and Leif catch Stephanie before she goes out on the deck, still giggling. Jon says to his sister, "Dad made these out of dark chocolate, so they're healthy for you."

"Great!" she replies, and she puts another one in her mouth. The men turn and chuckle as they walk into the living room. Al sees this and he walks into the living room and asks them, "What's so funny?"

Leif replies, "Dad put a stool softener in those chocolates to see who is stealing them."

Al looks at them and laughs profusely and the boys join in. "WTF? I just ate three of them—they're delicious."

"Y'all are sick bastards. I don't know who's the worst," Trace says licking her lips and holding her stomach.

Downtown Mason. There is the squealing of tires and the sound of busting glass. The two-tone slate-grey Pantera is racing through the city. Two police cars are chasing it and it has just gone through four red lights. Two vehicles are forced to collide and one rolls into a tree. The silver Corvette drifts around the corner into the driver's side of the police car that was in the front of the chase. The police cruiser forces its way beside the Corvette on the right as they come up to a left-hand turn. The cruiser forces the Corvette into the tall grass behind a small group of trees. The Corvette smashes its left front wheel off a picnic table with a family of four seated around it, sending the family flying through the air. The car does five rotations before coming to rest in a foot of water in the lake.

Two of the cruisers continue to chase the Pantera while one of them stops to check on the occupant in the Corvette and the family that has been hit. Officer Herbert jumps out of his cruiser and runs up to the open driver's door. With his gun raised, in an agitated tone, he yells, "Hands up, pecker head!" He looks up and radios in to the other officers, "Nope . . . whoever was driving the 'Vette is gone."

The two officers in pursuit of the Pantera are now talking back and forth on the radio. One states, "I've never seen anyone able to drive like this." Just then, a Ford SUV pulls up the hill, slicing through traffic, careening off parked cars. It sideswipes a pickup truck, tossing it on its side like a toy. Boxes of cherries shoot up into the air. Blood-red cherry juice splatters the intersection like a death-scene canvas. Cherries continue to roll in all directions. The Pantera is nowhere in sight. The police officers are boxed in as the wheels on the overturned truck slowly come to a stop. The driver of the truck stands on the curb, injured and shaking his head. The red-and-blue lights from the top of the cruisers reflect off the undercarriage of the fruit truck. An officer asks assertively, as the policemen get out of the cruisers, "Is anyone hurt?" The gentleman on the curb just shakes his head no. Bright green antifreeze carries cherries down the road between the officer's legs, like tiny canoes on a river.

Wondering what has happened with his car, Odan sits for a moment on the bench at the foot of his bed looking forward and holding an object in his hand. His two dogs are at his feet. Trace walks in hesitantly after knocking faintly on the door. He's looking straight ahead and says nothing.

"Are you all right?"

"I'm not sure," he replies.

She gets within five feet of him, and four of his grandchildren plus Ryker run past her and jump on him on the bed. The item that Odan was holding falls to the floor on the opposite side of the bed. It makes the sound of a metal object landing on short carpeting. Ryker gives Trace a disapproving look. Odan cracks a smile and tickles Ryker until he giggles and says, "Give me a bit, I'll be out there shortly."

Whining, the grandchildren reluctantly leave. Ryker is the last to go. Intentionally, but not hard, Ryker steps on Trace's foot as he walks out. Odan says in a stern voice, "Ryker." The children run outside onto the patio deck and then down below and play on the trampoline overlooking the lake.

Trace looks up and says, "What was that all about?"

He replies, "It just takes time." He leans to the far side of the bed and retrieves the object. He doesn't try to conceal it, nor does he make it obvious.

In a deliberate tone, looking straight at him she asks, "What is that?"

He looks down at the object, turning it in his hands. She walks closer and he stands up. He says in a heavy voice, "My biological mother gave it to me many years ago. It's a talisman. The other night, during the break-in, it was on the floor. It had a small key in the back. Mom said that if I was ever at the end of my rope, the key would open something close to home. But I never did. I never opened it. My mom's passed away, so now that I've lost the key, I'll never know what it was." He continues slowly, "I think it was given to my mom back in the seventies. I know less than nothing about my parents—my biological ones. I was planning to take some time this year to look into my genealogy, but then the little guy came along and now he pretty much takes up all my time, along with all the other things I'm doing."

He starts walking to the door and notices Kelly in the doorway. Kelly looks right past him at Trace. "How long have you been standing there?" Odan asks.

He replies, "Not long enough," with a short smile. They meet at the doorway. They do a friendly bump with their knuckles. Kelly walks back through the living room and through the nano doors onto the deck. Al, Jon and Leif follow Stephanie out onto the deck, giggling. They watch Stephanie pass out the chocolates and continue to smirk.

She's talking amongst the group and she states, "Do you know my dad's got a buddy in his bathroom?"

Leif grabs his belly and adds in a jolly tone, "You mean a bidet?"

"I don't know . . . that's what your brother told me," Stephanie replies.

"Which brother? Neil?" Jon asks.

"Yeah, I thought that's what he said," she replies.

Seven fifteen p.m. Brian is looking at his watch. He notices that Gary has left and Peter and his wife are getting up from the table. He's frustrated and tired of waiting. He has a disappointed look on his face as he gets up and goes to pay the bill. The two agents who were at his office earlier that day meet him at the front door of the restaurant.

The taller, younger man says in a sterile tone, "Your city is unravelling and you have no clue what's going on, do you?"

The older man turns to the young man and says, "How the hell is he supposed to know anything if no one tells him anything? Come outside," he says. "May I call you Brian?"

Brian says nothing, just nods his head holding the folder in his right hand, and they walk outside. Two additional bearded men walk over from opposite directions. Neither one of them is dressed in uniform; in fact, one of them is wearing sandals, shorts and a ripped T-shirt. They form a small circle and Brian becomes visibly agitated.

He asks, "What's this all about?"

"There are people out there that shouldn't be here, but because your sister started some shit, we can't fix it."

"I haven't got a clue what you're talking about," Brian says.

One of the men replies, "There's a woman who has been detained for a long time who is out now and she's causing some serious damage. And we have reason to believe it's all connected to Odan's family."

"What?" Brian asks, feigning disbelief.

The older agent says, "You know it, you just don't want to admit it. But because you're so naïve, I'll tell you a couple things that you need to know if you're going to fix this shit and catch your killer . . . Odan's biological father was one of the best researchers that this government or any government has ever seen. Period."

They walk to their respective vehicles and Brian turns to them and asks, "What the hell does a researcher have to do with people dying?"

There is the sound of quail running through the bushes nearby. After a long delay, the bearded man dressed in a ripped T-shirt says in a condescending tone, "Time kills us all and secrets bury us. Time has run out for a lot of people here. Their secrets have caught up with them . . . I think Odan has been carrying the burden of a lot of secrets and he has a drawer full of watches."

The other man walks up to Brian and hands him a key fob. Brian closes his fist around it and doesn't look at it. The men walk to their vehicles slowly. They all drive away, leaving Brian standing in the parking lot, staring down at the key fob in his closed fist and the folder in his other hand. On the drive home, the fob slides down the folder onto the seat. The fob has a crack all the way through it and it flips on its face. Brian notices that it's for Odan's Corvette.

Kuusamo. It's getting late. Two men are standing talking with each other near the front door. One of the men is in his thirties, six feet tall and attractive, with long black hair and an eight-day-old beard. The other man, Trace recognizes as Raymond. She goes over and introduces herself. "Hi, I'm Trace. I don't believe we've had the pleasure of meeting."

"I saw you briefly at the diner once . . . oh, look at the time. The wife is waiting for me. Will you excuse me? Hopefully we can see each other again soon," Raymond replies looking at his watch.

"No problem, lots of time," Trace says. Raymond nods his head and hustles out the door, waving at Odan. Odan gestures to him and Raymond freezes in the doorway. "The pleasure is all mine," says the other man who was with Raymond, nodding to Trace as he gets ready to leave also.

"I'm sorry, I don't think I caught your name," she says.

"It's M.C. I'm Odan's physician," he says with a smooth, subtle accent.

She asks, "Where is that accent from, if you don't mind me asking?"

With a smile, he says, "Pretoria, South Africa. Unfortunately, I must be leaving now, too. I have a wife and two spoiled children to deal with," he says as he waves and walks out the door.

Trace notices Odan has left for the deck and Raymond remains stationary by the doorway. Raymond turns to the doctor as they both exit the house and Trace hears him say, "She has no idea."

Raymond nods his head slowly. The rest of the barbecue passes by quickly with lots of laughter, good food and cocktails. Families and friends leave to go home. Ryker is put to bed. Odan and Kelly are out on the deck with a drink in hand when Trace walks up to them. She asks, "Everybody's gone. Do you need a hand cleaning up?"

Odan says, "No, no. It's fine," and she walks away, letting the two men finish their conversation. She walks through the house, looking at pictures and playing with the dial on the stereo. "Dreamweaver" comes on and she turns the volume up while looking over her shoulder to see if it is bothering the men. The dogs stride quietly out of the living room onto the deck and lie down beside the men.

Trace sits in front of the fireplace then, seeing the men still talking, she slowly gets up and walks toward the opening of the master bedroom. She hesitates for a moment and then presses on. She pulls her cell phone out of her pocket and sends a text to Odan from his bedroom. Her text reads:

I'm just going to lie down for a minute in your bed before I head out. Is that OK?

He replies with a smile emoji. She sits on his raised king bed which has a black, gold and brown quilt on it. She removes her shorts to reveal a red thong. Her thoughts and emotions are confused. She walks over to his closet and riffles through the shirts that are hanging there. She removes her blouse and pulls one of his white T-shirts over her naked top. She leaves her own shirt in the corner of his closet and walks slowly back to the bed, glancing out the doorway to the deck. She removes her small studded earrings and places them on the nightstand. Then she crawls into the bed that doesn't have a top sheet. The alcohol she's consumed has gotten to her, and she falls asleep within minutes.

Kelly says to Odan, "I've got to get some shut eye so I'll have to call this a night."

The two men walk toward the front door. Kelly says, "Make sure she gets home safe."

Odan grins as he opens the door and says, "Well, at least there are no cops here tonight." The men shake hands as the dogs come inside and lie down by the fireplace. Kelly leaves and closes the door behind him.

Odan walks around, picking up some odds and ends that have been scattered about and taking them to the kitchen. He looks at the opening to his bedroom. His mind is wrestling with whether to let her stay or not. He spends another half an hour cleaning up. Then he returns to the deck and leans over the railing. His thoughts are all about the little blue-eyed boy sleeping in the room a few feet away. His lack of a personal life is justified because of his decision to focus on Ryker.

After a minute, he walks up the stairs to the turret and looks out over the lake. He has so many questions running through his head. He looks at the wall and the pictures of his family and friends. He unclips his cell phone and puts it on the charger. Then he goes down to the main floor and walks to the door of his boy's bedroom and sees Ryker asleep. He adjusts the covers, then he leaves the room and gently closes the door, leaving an eight-inch gap.

He then walks over to his bedroom and sees Trace lying there, facing him on her left side. Her painted toenails on her foot with the ankle bracelet are peeking out from under the quilt. For the first time in a long time, he is truly indecisive as he walks around the bed to the other side. He takes in the sight of her earrings beside the bed. He walks over and grabs a pair of sweatpants off the shelf on the right-hand side of his walk-in closet. He removes his clothing, excluding his shorts, and puts on the sweatpants. He then walks back over to the bed, pulls back the cover gently and climbs in.

He sees that she is wearing one of his T-shirts and red panties. He slides over within twelve inches of her, and gently touches her with his fingertips on the small of her back with his hand, then turns over to lie on his back. He tries to sleep, but he is in and out of consciousness all night.

At four in the morning, Odan looks over to see Ryker. The little boy crawls into his bed. Ryker grabs Odan's hand and sticks his little fist in it. Odan turns to see his face and closes his palm. Odan falls back to sleep, listening to the rhythm of Trace's and Ryker's breath.

Thirty miles east, inside a garage, a man is working on the rear engine of the grey Pantera. There is a twenty-three-foot sleek black aluminum jet boat beside it on a trailer. The man stands up and he says to a woman not in view, "There's blood in here, and what do you expect me to do with the bullet hole in the fender?"

"Just patch up the car, make it look good and don't worry about the blood, it's mine," she replies. She walks out of the shadows. The two work on the car through the night.

Kuusamo. The sun pokes through the low-hanging clouds. It's seven-thirty a.m., and morning has broken. Trace wakes up and finds she's in bed alone. She sits up and runs her hands through her hair. She walks over to the mirror on the dresser, and gently rubs her fingers under her eyes and says nothing. She looks down at the T-shirt she's wearing and realizes it's just barely long enough to cover her underwear. The puppies have come into the room and do a U-turn behind her as she walks out of the bedroom, through the living room and into the kitchen. The little blond-haired boy sits at the island in the kitchen in his banana pyjamas, eating a bowl of oatmeal. Odan enters the kitchen and turns away from her across the counter.

Trace asks, "Where did you sleep last night?"

Without answering, Odan asks her, "How did you sleep?"

She says, "Great, the best I've slept in years."

Ryker pipes up, "Dyno slept with you."

There is silence for thirty seconds and she says, "What?"

Ryker replies, "Dyno slept beside you last night, and I slept beside Dyno."

Odan has a smile. He's hiding from her. Trace has a look of guilt on her face mixed with her small-town-girl smile, and then she bites her lip.

Morning is in full stride and Brian is out running when he gets a phone call. "You're not gonna believe this but we found two more bodies," the voice on the other end says.

Brian stops. "We found a woman in a bathtub of wine down at the Racoon Motel, and now I'm out at Odan's waste site, and there's a lady's body that's on the top of a sea can that's three cans high."

Brian replies, "Do we know who they are? And how the hell did a body get at the top of three sea cans?"

The officer replies, "Lisa Jackson is the name of the vic that was found in the Racoon Motel, and—"

Brian finishes his sentence for him. "Catarina Wanderbelt is the other one."

"Yes, how did you know?" asks the officer.

Brian goes on to say, "They were both supposed to meet me at the restaurant last night and they never showed. What is the cause of death for Wanderbelt?"

The officer replies, "We're not quite sure. Gravity. There's a big dent in the top of the can so it looks like she fell from the sky."

Brian's thoughts drift back to the cell phone. He jogs back to his SUV and climbs in. He drives straight to his parents' place. He finds himself driving erratically as his mind bounces back in time, between being fifteen and his job now. He tries to put all the pieces together regarding his parents' involvement in the atrocities occurring around town. What kind of crepuscular creatures were at work here? Why would his laidback parents be mixed up in this? And most important, why didn't he see any of it coming?

11

Talisman

Brian pulls up to his parents' house and gets out at his old home. Both his parents are sitting on the veranda. As he takes the stairs, he blurts out, "Cut through the shit. What do you guys know about Odan's parents? I don't want my own parents lying to me and I have to know how you are involved in this shit, be it in any shape or form."

His mom puts her hand on her husband's knee and pats it, then stands up. "Let's go inside, son," she says, and continues to talk quietly as they walk in the house.

"I was friends with his mother," she states, "many years ago, before things started to happen."

"What kinds of things?" Brian asks.

"She was an athlete and the government recruited her because she had certain skills," his mom says.

"Who are we talking about and what skills?" Brian asks, confused.

"She made friends in every circle and she just seemed to blend in . . . and disappear. There wasn't one thing she wasn't good at—not that I know of, anyway. Back then, she could run a marathon, shoot a rifle, kill a fox at two hundred yards, win a NASCAR race, and drink a glass of wine with a foreign dignitaries while carrying on a conversation in their native tongue all on the same day."

Brian asks, his voice escalating, "Who *is* she?" He turns around and slams his hand into the wall, knocking a picture down to the floor.

"That's not important," she replies. "The important part is she called me days ago and asked me where the talisman was. I told her that I had given it to Odan in nineteen seventy-four. She asked me before she disappeared to give the artifact to the woman who adopted him, and I did. I hadn't heard from her for all these years, up until the other night."

"Mom . . . dammit! Don't you think I should've known this a long time ago? I've got a dead judge's cell phone with a dead drug dealer's blood on it . . . calling you in the middle of night." He shakes his head and starts to walk out of the house.

When Brian reaches the door, his mother says, "Don't you want to know what she asked me?"

He stops as he's pushing the door open and looks over his left shoulder. His eyes are open wide as he waits for her response.

"Odan has the talisman. She just asked me if I fulfilled my promise to pass it over to him. Now, the mother who raised him has been dead since nineteen eighty-five, and I assumed he's had it all this time. I don't really know anything about it. I didn't say anything when I handed it to her, and she never asked me any questions."

Brian asks, "Do you have any guesses as to what it's all about?"

His mom turns without answering him and walks into the kitchen. His father is quiet, still sitting on the swing on the veranda. Brian goes outside. "Dad, cut me some slack. This is bullshit and you know it, so tell me what I need to know, right now, goddammit!"

Before his father can answer his question, Brian looks around and says, "And where the hell is Trace?"

"She went out to a barbecue at Odan's last night and didn't come home," says Arthur, very quietly, his voice almost a whisper. Arthur stands up and starts walking away, down the steps and across the lawn toward the orchard. Brian follows.

"You see, it's like this," Arthur explains. "The government was in a big hiring mode and they were looking for people with specific talents and your mother's friend was someone they were interested in for a long time. I think that they got to her when she was in high school and they played her, drugged her even. I don't know anyone else who got the scholarships she did back then. It was really odd, because they even gave your mother a scholarship to keep her close, in case something like this happened."

Brian says, "This stuff doesn't happen in the real world. Are we talking about spies here? I don't . . ."

He doesn't finish his sentence. Brian and Arthur stand facing each other beside a cherry tree. Brian continues, "Why *my* family? And why am I only learning this now, after all these years?"

He walks away from his dad, back to his SUV, shaking his head gently. His mom is standing on the porch with her arms crossed and watches as he drives away. He sits and thinks about the thirty-plus people who lied, testified against Odan. They have no idea of their fate, not to mention that the judges and district attorneys were on the take.

Back at Kuusamo, Odan has the little boy dressed. He says, "I can meet you in forty-five minutes at Starbucks, if that works for you?"

Trace replies from another room, "Are you talking to me?"

"Yes, I am. I have to drop the little guy off and then I can grab a coffee with you. I'll try to rearrange my day if you're interested in spending some time with me," he says as his heart skips.

"I'd love that. May I use your shower?" she asks.

"Knock yourself out. I'll turn the cameras off when I get home," he says jokingly. She replies, "You're a funny guy. See ya there."

She can hear Ryker saying repeatedly, "Dyno, Dyno, Dyno, Dyno," as Odan goes out the door to his truck.

When she hears his truck drive away, she opens the nano doors to the deck. It's already seventy-two degrees and a warm south-east breeze cascades off the lake and onto her face. She walks onto the deck and takes her panties off from under the T-shirt and walks with them hung on her finger as she walks through the empty home toward the shower in his bedroom. She hears her cell phone vibrate and she goes over to it and notices three missed calls from her brother. She ignores them and pulls Odan's T-shirt over her head as she walks toward the shower.

In the marble shower, she notices a rainforest shower head and multiple handhelds on the beautiful marble walls. She enjoys the shower, and takes her time, slowly moving one of the handheld nozzles from her toes up her leg to her inner thigh. She notices a black button on the wall and pushes it. Her eyes light up as a narrow fountain of warm water sprays up out of the floor. After a brief pause, she positions herself over the fountain and places her palms on the steamy glass. It takes her away, possibly thinking of the homeowner.

Five hundred miles away at 15,000 feet in the air, Peter Derickson and his wife are on a jet. They're flying away on a trip the day after they had supper at The Lizard and Chicken.

The woman says to her husband, "It's funny because the trip only included a one-way ticket for you . . . but I decided to pay the balance because it seemed like it was just a misunderstanding."

Puzzled, Peter looks at his wife and says, "I think I got some sort of food poisoning at the restaurant last night because I'm feeling really shitty right now."

A flight attendant comes by and notices he's turning white. She grabs a medic from the front of the plane. The tall male medic follows the attendant. Peter falls over into the centre of the aisle of the plane.

The medic asks, "Any medical conditions?"

Peter's wife replies, "Yes, he has a pacemaker."

A yellow pencil falls out of the medic's pocket onto the floor. Peter rolls over on his side, vomits and goes unconscious. The attendants wrap him in a blanket and carry him to the rear of the plane.

The attendant comes back to Peter's wife and says, "We're so sorry . . . our medical supplies are inexplicably not on board." Then the pilot comes over the speaker and states that the plane will need to land at the nearest airport for emergency medical reasons.

"Oh my God !" Peter's wife gasps.

Just as they're about to land, the medic says, "We may have been able to save him, but his tattoo bracelet said 'Do not resuscitate.'"

In shock, she replies, "That's not what it says."

Brian gets a call from the office. He reluctantly answers it. The officer on the other line says, "We've got two more. That Bart guy on the walkway by the lake—"

Brian stops him. "I know, and I just heard Peter Derickson died on an airplane that's landing in Reno," Brian says.

Odan sits patiently at the Starbucks waiting for Trace. He's sitting up against the glass with two coffees waiting on the table. Two women sit down who are about to start their shift. One is Renee and the other is Brodie. They are both young, attractive baristas. They ask where Ryker is.

Odan replies, "He's at kindergarten today. I pick him up at three o'clock." The older one, Renee, asks, "Where is his family?"

"It's complicated, but this is what I can tell you. His father has passed away and his mother is in the hospital in a coma. His uncle was a small-time drug dealer who was just found murdered. I was in love with his grandmother. The problem is, she didn't know how to love me back."

Renee says, "I'm sorry to hear that. I thought it was something totally different." Brodie asks, "Where is Jon, your son, today?"

With a smile he replies, "You do know he's got the hots for you."

Her cheeks flush and she says, "He's all right. He always smiles at me."

Odan leans back in his chair. "He always has some laundry to do after he sees you."

She smiles a confused smile at him and the women get up and put on their aprons then head behind the counter. Trace walks in, followed by a bearded man who goes over and sits in the corner. Another man from his table, also with a beard, gets up and gets in line to order drinks.

Trace walks directly over to Odan and notices the coffee sitting on the table waiting for her. "Thank you," she says, "just what a girl needs to start her day, after a relaxing shower."

Odan looks over at the bearded man and then brushes off his paranoia.

Trace asks Odan, "What's your plan for the day?"

He replies, "I thought this was going to be our day to hang out until three o'clock. Why don't you leave your car here. You can come with me and, because your brother is the chief of police, I'm sure that if your car is here that prick won't have it towed."

She stands up and says, "Be nice . . . he's under a lot of stress these days."

He stands up and replies, "That's true. I just wish he wasn't such a prick to me." "There you go again. Can you try to finish a sentence without swearing?" Trace asks.

"Oh great!" he says. "You spent one night in my bed and you're already telling me what to do." They both smile. He walks by with the triangle of his arm extended for her to grab and she takes it. He slows his gait as they approach the door and the two bearded men. He stops and leans over toward the younger one and, with a smile, he says, "Just in case you're wondering, we're changing vehicles in fifteen minutes so you better keep up."

The two gentlemen look at each other and the older one smiles back, but before the door closes, he says to Odan, "How do you know we're not watching your back?" With a wink, Odan replies, "Because you're on my ass."

Trace and Odan continue out the door. They disconnect at the elbow as soon as they have exited the door. They both walk toward his truck and she looks over at him twice during the fifty-foot walk. He cuts in front of her to open her door. Then he closes it behind her as he looks over his shoulder at the two men still seated in the restaurant. He puts on his sunglasses which were resting on the dashboard, and he pushes the Start button. He continues to stare at the men, until they leave the coffee shop and get in their tan SUV. He looks over at her and smiles and says, "I guess it's showtime."

He pulls away, driving slowly until he gets on Railway Avenue. Once the men are directly behind him, he nails the throttle and the truck accelerates sideways and doesn't straighten out until it reaches sixty miles an hour. The supercharger is whining as the gears are leaned on.

Trace shrieks, grabbing the door and her seat. The truck pulls farther and farther away from the two men following it. Finally, around the corner, they turn a sharp right heading south, passing a 720 McLaren and the men following them and go straight.

With a concerned look on her face, she yells at him, "Don't go any farther! What's this about! You're a fuckin' idiot!"

He pulls over and puts the truck in Park and takes his sunglasses off and tosses them on the armrest between them. "Think about it. They followed you into the coffee shop. And what's more, as soon as I drop you off today, this article of yours is over with."

Her voice breaking, she asks, "Did you ever think *why* they wanted me to do an article on you? Or did you really think this was all coincidence?"

He looks down and takes a moment, looking forward, then leans toward her and asks, "What do you suggest we do? We're sitting here on the side of the road. One or both of us is being followed. My house has been gone through. People I don't trust are dying all around me. We have to do something about this. We need to back up a bit and figure out what it is they want or who they want. Apparently they're not the Red Cross looking for donations. We can solve this . . . after all, you're supposed to be some hotshot investigative reporter."

She powers down her window and says, "Fine. Let's go through with it. We have to find out what they're after. We need to ride this out."

He sighs, leans back and says with a crack in his voice, "You know I spent the better part of ten years worrying whether they were gonna put me away for something I didn't do. Then it dawned on me. Over the last year and a half, the only thing I've been concerned about is what would happen to Ryker if they ever got me. That's messed up, because I'm focused on a little boy who's not mine because *he* made *me* his. I have very little fight left in me . . . unless it's for him. Don't get me wrong. My kids are grown up now but I still love them, but it really gets in my head when we talk about Ryker. I have a son who believes that what I feel for Ryker is pseudo-love. But it is more real than anyone will ever know."

He puts the truck in Drive and starts away from the curb and says, "Because of the circumstances, we need to change our wheels . . . oh, and did I hear you had a . . . relaxing shower?"

She smiles at him and puts her hand on the centre console and he grabs her thumb and gives it a gentle squeeze. "Let's go," he says. They drive to the airport and park the truck in the hangar. He instructs her to go get in the green car. Then he says, "I have to go grab something. I'll be right there." He returns to find, to his surprise, she's not in the green car but is in the passenger seat of his brand-new black-and-silver Stepchild Mustang.

She waits for him. In a couple of minutes, he arrives at the car and climbs in behind the wheel. He puts a two-tone grey nine-inch box beside his seat and plugs it into the dashboard.

"What's that?" she asks.

He replies with a smile, "It's a monitor. We can listen to every firefighter and cop in the country with this baby.

This little button controls the frequency and if you look on the side, there's actually a handle just like the police."

Brian is driving to the nearby town of Kirkheld to check out the lead when he receives a radio call from the station, from one of his officers. The officer states, "You're not gonna believe this. We've got a lead on the boat seen out by Odan's. There was a complaint about a loud black river boat being pulled out of the water two miles up the shoreline from the big guy's place."

"Go ahead," says Brian, as he pushes the mic to talk.

"It was over twenty feet long and witnesses saw it being pulled out of the water at one o'clock in the morning on that same night as the break-in. But here's the funny thing. The trailer that pulled the boat was registered to the government back in the seventies. It appears no one's ever changed the plates. That's the reason it stuck out."

Brian asks, "Were they able to actually catch the plate number?"

The voice on the other end of the radio says, "Yeah. It appears the trailer belongs to DND. It's an antique, Chief, but the plate is still active."

Brian replies, "I guess that'll be a dead end because they're almost impossible to get anything out of."

"Not exactly," the officer says. "The plate was picked up in the seventies by a woman."

Brian replies, "I'm not surprised. We've been one step behind this female since day one."

There's a hesitation and the officer comes back on the radio, "The plate was picked up by someone matching your mother's description forty years ago."

There is dead silence and Brian drops the radio receiver.

Brian pulls into his house and opens the garage door and reveals an orange Shelby Mustang. He walks up to it and opens the door. He climbs in gingerly. The key swings slowly as the door closes behind him. He feels the eyes and ears of the valley on him and his old friend.

Odan turns the volume down on his two-way radio and pushes a button on the dash to have it come through the stereo. Just then he hears a call.

"We're currently involved in a high-speed chase between that Pantera, a tan-coloured SUV and a black Dodge Challenger. A black Dodge Challenger Hellcat was stolen from the dealership early this morning."

Odan pushes the Start button on the car and squeals his tires as he leaves the hangar. He grabs a radio and focuses on the road as Trace does up her seat belt.

"Those were the same furry-faced guys who were in the SUV following us," Trace says.

Odan replies, "Good chance." He slams the car around the first left turn coming out of the airport. The talisman slides out from between the passenger seat and the centre console. He looks up at her and says, "Why the hell did you bring that and what are you doing with it anyways?"

Trace replies, "It was sitting on your dresser and I turned it over and I found some numbers inscribed on it. I thought you might like to see."

Just then Brian comes over the radio, "Odan, I know you can hear me. Stay out of this. I'm going to catch them right now."

He fires up the Shelby and spins his tires as he leaves the garage. On the radio, they both hear that the cars are approaching the corner of 49th and 23rd. Brian says, "I got this, my friend."

Odan replies, "You used to be my friend and I hope I can trust you, but, just the same . . . I'm not letting them go." Odan presses a button on his receiver and says to his pilot, Tom, "Do you have your ears on?"

"Affirmative," Tom replies, as he sits listening to the sound of the Cessna's engine.

"We're looking for a black car, a tan SUV coming up on forty-nine and twenty-three. Can you swing over and take a bird's-eye view?" Odan asks in an assertive voice.

"That's a ten-four, Boss. I'm three or four minutes out and I'm full of fuel," Tom replies.

Odan can feel her heart race, and before he can say anything, she interrupts him and grabs his right wrist. "What if those numbers on the back of the talisman are part of a GPS coordinate?" Trace asks.

"And what if," he replies in a sarcastic tone, "they are forty years old, maybe older." He continues, "Trust me, most properties have been subdivided or redeveloped by now.

"But what if your mom wanted you to find this?" Trace says, while looking at him with concern, placing her hand high on his thigh.

He replies, "You didn't know my mom. She wouldn't have done something like that. She was a straightforward meat-and-potatoes kinda lady and was kind as the day is long."

Trace replies as she puts the talisman down, "I'm talking about your biological mom."

The car revs up as he passes two more trucks on the left-hand side. Tom comes over the two-way radio. "That orange Mustang isn't far behind them now and there are cops on route. Make up some time."

"The Stepchild is now approaching the rear of the orange Shelby," Trace says on the two-way. "We can see you. We're right behind you."

Brian replies, "What the hell are you doing here, Trace?"

"I was being followed and now I'm not. Someone's been fucking with you since day one—can't you see that?" she says.

"Hey, Brian, think it's time you follow me. After all, that's what you've been doing ever since I left the first time," Odan says, passing the mic to Trace as he drifts past the third last car between him and Brian.

"You and your tin can, you got nothing on me," Brian says over his Bluetooth radio in a brotherly tone.

"Well, I guess it's time to feed that little pony some protein, because you don't know your cars. I'm all motor. Your Shelby is about to meet the fury of the Stepchild and I'm running a thousand screaming My Little Ponies," says Odan smugly. He smiles gently at Trace as he's closing in on the group of vehicles. "You can read me the numbers on the back of the talisman," he states in a humble tone.

She starts to read the numbers out loud, "Fifty-one . . . something, one hundred and nineteen . . . something."

"Stop, stop, stop. I know where that is," he replies. He continues, "I was taken there a very . . . very long time ago.

I'm not sure exactly how old I was." He elevates his voice and asks Tom on the two-way, "Can you follow them? I'm splitting off." Odan has an epiphany. He looks at Trace.

Trace says, "The fight . . . it's my guess that whoever is up there in that car is trying to lead people away from where we're going."

Brian glances back in the rearview mirror and notices that the Stepchild is gone. Brian asks over the radio, "Are you guys okay?" in a concerned tone.

Odan replies, "More than fine, good buddy . . . it's your chase. We'll keep you posted on this end."

Driving at the speed limit, the two of them are taking the Stepchild down through the valley and then up over the crest.

"Where are you taking me?" she asks.

"There are two places that my mom used to take me when I was little and one of them was not far from Knox Mountain," he replies, "halfway to Fintree."

Brian comes on the radio and says, "It appears we've lost her."

Odan replies, "I'm not surprised."

"She drives a lot like you . . . or like you used to."

Trace says, "Maybe he drives like her for a reason."

Tom comes back on the radio and says, "I have no idea what happened. Those two cars just disappeared, that Pantera and then that black Hellcat."

"Keep looking until you have fuel issues," Odan instructs him and Tom replies, "Affirmative." They drive on and reach a turn-off that's called "Joseph Rich." They turn left and start climbing a winding road. The asphalt slowly turns to dirt. As soon as they turn right, they notice the black Charger parked on the side of the road at the entrance to Woody Nook Road.

"'The 'Vette has been stolen from the compound and the tan SUV has crashed . . . there is no one inside," a voice says over the radio. Trace and Odan drive slowly as the road turns into barely a path. Leaves crackle under the tires as the Stepchild crawls slowly over the narrowing trail. Its spoiler is parting grass blades and picking up twigs. Trace looks at Odan and says, "Shouldn't we be calling someone?"

He looks at her, smiles and puts his right hand on her left knee, then says in a reserved tone, "She's already here and it's not gonna make any difference."

Trace looks down and grabs her cell phone and sends a text message off to her brother. The message fails to send.

Odan replies, "Do you really think there's cell phone coverage out here?"

They pull up to a forty-by-forty shop. The sun-faded brown doors are open. The black Pantera that everybody's been chasing, a black boat and a black motorcycle sit inside. They can see a barn past the shop, about one hundred and fifty feet away. They exit the car slowly and close the doors quietly. *Click.* They walk into the shop, with Odan in the lead and Trace following. She feels her beating heart in her throat. She takes her left hand and puts a finger through the belt loop on his pants.

He turns to her and an unexpected sense of home comes over him. He attempts to calm her nerves with a smile and says quietly, "Are you sure you're not related to Ryker?"

As they walk through the shop he does not seem to be concerned, but Trace is overwhelmed. She says, "In case we don't make it out of here, I thought I'd better tell you, I find you very attractive, even sexy."

He replies, "That's not the first time I've heard that, but I'm sure the last girl who said it was looking in my wallet, not hanging on to my belt loop."

They walk around the perimeter of the car and the boat and head out the opening, turning right when they've cleared it. They start up the path toward the barn. Italian plum and raspberry bushes flank the path. He says, "I lived here for a year when I graduated from high school. There used to be a mobile home between the shop and the barn. Your brother was my best friend back then."

In a puzzled voice, she says, "I've never heard him talk about this or even you." As he walks, he mumbles, "Why would anyone want to do this to me? I haven't been up here in years."

They enter the barn and in the shadows of the hayloft there is a woman tied to a wooden chair seventy feet in front of them. The barn is poorly lit but there is light that shines through from a missing board in the centre. As they get closer, Trace pulls harder on Odan's belt loop. A shadow comes appears under the hayloft behind the woman seated in the chair. As it enters the light, Trace sees that it is a woman. She holds a book in her left hand and a gun in her right. The woman with the gun says, "Lose the girl."

"No!" Trace says. The woman with gun turns and points it at Trace, and then slowly turns it one hundred and eighty degrees clockwise and points it at the girl tied up in the chair. The woman with the gun takes two more steps forward and Odan notices his ledger in her left hand. The woman fires at the woman sitting in the chair. Just as the shot rings out, two more shots are fired from behind them over Odan's shoulder.

Odan and Trace drop to the ground. The pair look up with caution. Odan's arms are shielding Trace. They kneel quietly as a man comes up behind them into view. He lowers his gun and stands directly to their right. The man is wearing a rune stone thumb ring. He looks over at the two and says, "Sorry," locking eyes with Odan. The sounds of Brian's Shelby rumbling up the laneway can be heard outside the barn.

Odan and Trace stand up and Trace asks, "Who are you?"

"My name is Hayden," the man states. The three walk over quickly to the woman who is shot and is still holding the gun. She is also holding Odan's diary. There's blood on her hand and covering the book.

Odan asks the man, "Who is she?"

Hayden pauses then says hesitantly, "Her name is Elon." He continues, "She's your mother and I am your father."

12

The Answer

A dozen police cars, four special investigative officers and two emergency vehicles are on site. The ambulances leave with Elon and Esme.

Brian walks up to Odan and says, "Do you know those women?"

Odan looks at his father and says to Brian, "The younger woman is Esme—she is the mother of my youngest son."

Brian sees the men looking at each other and says, "It doesn't look like either one of them are going to make it." Then he says to Hayden, "I have all your credentials, but you're still going to have to come down and answer some questions."

Hayden looks back at Brian and says, "No, I'm not. My boss will be here within the hour."

"If you refuse to cooperate, I'm going to have to slap the cuffs on you and take you down there myself," Brian states.

"You're an elected official. It's a good chance that you'll be looking for work tomorrow at this time," says an agent who walks up behind him. Brian and the agent walk away and leave Hayden and Odan to talk.

Hayden explains, "I met your mother many years ago. Our jobs were different. My job was, and is, strictly to collect information and follow reports. Your mother's, on the other hand, was totally different. She had a trade name. She was specially earmarked as a Tour Guide, and that meant her responsibility was to get people in and out of tight spots. She has rescued a lot of kidnapped victims in her time."

He continues as they walk down the pathway. "Her first job was to get some people, including myself, out of Europe. It was simple. She helped me and then we fell in love and here you are."

Odan asks, "Why all this and why now?"

"The government tried to sweep it—and her—under the rug," Hayden answers, "They wanted her to get rid of the baby because it didn't fit their plan. Then she went on a couple of missions with some bad people and she decided not to bring them back. She learned a lot of skills over the years, but when they caught up to her, they locked her away. It wasn't until Trace posted information about you that she knew exactly what you were doing and where you were."

"What?" Odan asked in a surprised tone.

Casually, Hayden explains, "Yeah, your adopted mother just thought it would be the right thing to do, to try to reunite you and your biological mother by getting one of her old employers to do some research. That set a whole slew of bells and whistles off, and led us to where we are today. I've been trying to follow her and stop her since the first day that she got out. I was around the corner, for that matter, the day that she went through all your stuff at your house found your diary. I guess she took it upon herself to right all your wrongs. I wish I could go back and fix things. I never thought it would go this far, and I trusted the people I thought had my back. They were doing a good job, but it wasn't until I got here that I realized all the shit you've been involved in. And I heard you've also been busy in the offspring department." He winks at Odan then.

"I can't change anything and I've never been father material,"Hayden continues. "But I am truly happy to meet you," he says with a real smile. "So where do we go from here?" Odan asks.

"It's your call. I have a little unfinished business to take care of, but if you want, we can stay in touch . . . and stay close," Hayden replies as he sheds a tear.

Odan asks, "Is it too much to ask if you can hang around a while, so I can ask you some more questions? Can I maybe buy you a coffee or something?"

"I don't think a coffee is going to cut it, but maybe one of those drinks you serve at your restaurant will," Hayden says with a smile.

"I'd love to buy you a drink," Odan says, "but first, I have to go and say sorry to a girl, and maybe ask her out on a real date."

Hayden replies, "How about I see you tomorrow at the restaurant. Oh, and one more thing," he says, as he holds up his hand. "This key belongs to you. It was the key on the back of the talisman and it unlocks the shop here. This property and everything on it belongs to you, and it always has."

Before he goes, Hayden raises one eyebrow. "I've gotta know . . . could she be the one?" he asks, looking at Trace.

Turning to look at the woman standing a few feet off to his right, and then gazing up at the sky, he replies, "Late the other night I heard her voice call me. I swear it was a prayer from the moon."

Two days later at the top of Knox Mountain, overlooking the city, four people are standing side by side: Kelly, with a crossbow in his left hand; Elon, with her arm in a sling; Dr. M.C.; and Channi on the far right.

Channi says, "This isn't over, is it?" as they hear the music coming from the restaurant down below.

Special thanks and acknowledgments:

Okanagan Aggregates Ltd., 1504 Blattner Road, Armstrong, BC

Fleet FX Graphics Inc., 17930, 105 Ave NW, Edmonton, AB

Thompson Cooper, Victoria, BC

The patience of all my family and friends. Ryker's love means everything.